# *Enrollment Form*

## ☐ *Yes!* I WANT TO BE A *P*RIVILEGED *W*OMAN.

Enclosed is one *PAGES & PRIVILEGES*™ Proof of Purchase from any Harlequin or Silhouette book currently for sale in stores (Proofs of Purchase are found on the back pages of books) and the store cash register receipt. Please enroll me in *PAGES & PRIVILEGES*™. Send my Welcome Kit and FREE Gifts -- and activate my FREE benefits -- immediately.

*More great gifts and benefits to come like these luxurious Truly Lace and L'Effleur gift baskets.*

---

**NAME (please print)**

---

**ADDRESS**                                                    **APT. NO**

---

**CITY**                        **STATE**                **ZIP/POSTAL CODE**

---

PROOF OF PURCHASE
*SAMPLE ONLY*

Please allow 6-8 weeks for delivery. Quantities are limited. We reserve the right to substitute items. Enroll before October 31, 1995 and receive one full year of benefits.

### *NO CLUB! NO COMMITMENT!*
Just one purchase brings you great **Free Gifts** and **Benefits!**

*(More details in back of this book.)*

---

Name of store where this book was purchased_____

Date of purchase_____

Type of store:

☐ Bookstore  ☐ Supermarket  ☐ Drugstore

☐ Dept. or discount store (e.g. K-Mart or Walmart)

☐ Other (specify)_____

Which Harlequin or Silhouette series do you usually read?

---

**Complete and mail with one Proof of Purchase and store receipt to:**

**U.S.:** *PAGES & PRIVILEGES*™, P.O. Box 1960, Danbury, CT 06813-1960

**Canada:** *PAGES & PRIVILEGES*™, 49-6A The Donway West, P.O. 813, North York, ON M3C 2E8          **PRINTED IN U.S.A**

# "What About Sex?" Sam Asked.

She swallowed. "What about it?"

"Don't play dumb, Curly." He let his thumbs trace the delicate line of her collarbone. "You know what I mean."

"Can't we cross that bridge when we come to it?"

Catching her waist, he jerked her up against him, bending to nuzzle the flower-fragrant crook of her neck. His unexpected touch evoked a shiver and a gasp from her, and he bared his teeth in a wolfish grin, muttering, "I think we just did."

"You're not going to scare me off, if that's what this is."

"A man wants a willing woman in his bed, Veronica Jean, not a martyr."

Her breathing accelerated, and she hesitated, licking her lips. "I—I'm not unwilling."

Dear Reader,

Imagine that you're single, and you've been longing for a family all your life…but there aren't any husband prospects in sight. Then suddenly, a handsome, sexy rancher offers you a proposition: marry him. The catch— you've got to help raise his four rambunctious children. It's tempting…but is it practical? That's the dilemma faced by Kara Kirby in this month's MAN OF THE MONTH, *The Wilde Bunch* by Barbara Boswell. What does Kara do? I'm not telling—you have to read the book!

And a new miniseries begins, MEN OF THE BLACK WATCH, with *Heart of the Hunter* by BJ James. The "Black Watch" is a top-secret organization whose agents face danger every day, but now face danger of a different sort—the danger of losing your heart when you fall in love.

In addition, the CODE OF THE WEST series continues with Luke's story in *Cowboys Don't Quit* by Anne McAllister. And the HEART OF STONE series continues with *Texas Temptation* by Barbara McCauley.

For a light, romantic romp don't miss Karen Leabo's *Man Overboard;* and a single dad gets saddled with a batch of babies in *The Rancher and the Redhead* by Suzannah Davis.

I hope you enjoy them all—I certainly do!

Lucia Macro
Senior Editor

Please address questions and book requests to:
Silhouette Reader Service
U.S.: 3010 Walden Ave., P.O. Box 1325, Buffalo, NY 14269
Canadian: P.O. Box 609, Fort Erie, Ont. L2A 5X3

# SUZANNAH DAVIS

## THE RANCHER AND THE REDHEAD

SILHOUETTE *Desire*®
Published by Silhouette Books
America's Publisher of Contemporary Romance

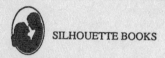

 SILHOUETTE BOOKS

ISBN 0-373-05947-7

THE RANCHER AND THE REDHEAD

**Books by Suzannah Davis**

Silhouette Desire

*A Christmas Cowboy* #903
*The Rancher and the Redhead* #947

---

## SUZANNAH DAVIS

Award-winning author Suzannah Davis is a Louisiana native who loves small-town life, daffodils and writing stories full of love and laughter. A firm believer in happy endings, she has three children. *The Rancher and the Redhead* is her sixteenth novel.

For my parents,
Gordon and Lynn Nelson

# One

*"Curly, get your fanny over here pronto! I need you."*

Sam Preston's ominous words echoed in her head as Roni Daniels floored the accelerator of her aging Jeep and bounced over the cattle gap leading into the Lazy Diamond Ranch. Gravel spewed, and she grappled white-knuckled at the steering wheel, trying to focus sleep-blurred eyes on the narrow track. The cool April air of a Texas midnight blew her dark curls into a wild tangle, and she cursed the rancher for jarring her out of a sound sleep, for making her forget her usual hair clip and for hanging up before explaining what disaster prompted his preemptory phone call.

But in this part of Texas, when a neighbor hollered in the middle of the night, a real friend didn't stop to ask questions. A real friend came a-running. *Pronto.*

Roni braked to a stop in front of the once-grand Preston ranch house. Her headlights revealed the peeling paint on the weathered siding, the sagging boards on the rambling porches. By contrast, all the outbuildings and barns were shipshape and letter perfect. But then, ever since his wife had left him five years earlier, Sam had cared more about the Brahma cattle he raised than his own comfort.

Vaulting from her seat, Roni raced up the front steps, her overactive artist's imagination conjuring visions of bloody mayhem, severe bodily injury or—at the very least—alien invaders. It took something dire and desperate to make self-sufficient Sam Preston yell for help!

"Sam!" Roni flung open the screen door and skidded into the lamplit front parlor. She'd been coming in and out of the Preston place for most of her thirty-four years, tagging along after Sam and his older brother Kenny since she was "knee-high to a grasshopper," as old Doc Hazelton liked to say. Now she looked askance at the explosion of boxes and suitcases and unidentifiable paraphernalia that turned the perennially tidy room into a combat zone.

Called out of town a few days ago, Sam had missed their usual Friday night with the other regulars down at Rosie's Café. But the life of a struggling cattleman and aspiring rodeo stock supplier was erratic, and Roni hadn't thought his absence anything unusual.

Apparently she'd been wrong. Very, very wrong.

"Sam, where are—"

A strident mewling from the rear of the house interrupted Roni's call and raised the hairs on the back of her neck. Heart thudding, she hurried down the hall to the master bedroom, then cautiously pushed open the door.

She'd expected ectoplasmic demons or chain-saw killers. What she found was even more alarming—Sam Preston, dripping wet and wearing only a towel. Sun-bleached blond hair plastered the brow of his familiar, craggy face, but it was the unexpected glimpse of bare, well-muscled

chest and lean horseman's thighs that made Roni suck in a
tiny involuntary breath. Then he swung to face her, and the
struggling bundle he cradled in his brawny arms made Roni
stop breathing altogether.

"Curly! Thank Jehoshaphat. Here!"

Sam thrust the squalling infant into Roni's grasp and
made a grab for the towel sliding dangerously south of his
navel. Dumbfounded, Roni had no choice but to juggle the
kicking, red-faced baby. The child—female by the pink
color of her gown—was about a year old and sported the
most extraordinary mop of russet-colored curls Roni had
ever seen. She was also enraged, and heavy and strong
enough to make holding her steady a struggle.

"Oh my God!" Roni automatically propped the baby
against her shoulder, too astonished to give more than cur-
sory notice to the dampness that immediately began to seep
through her T-shirt. Startled by a new voice, the child broke
off her caterwauling, unscrewed her rosebud face and
looked solemnly up at Roni...with Sam's very own bluebonnet eyes.

Shock slammed into the center of Roni's chest, a pierc-
ing pain that was part dismay, part hurt mortification. How
could he have kept something like this from her, from his
very best friend in the world?

"Turn your back, Curly, so I can get on my skivvies." As
Roni automatically looked away, Sam rummaged in an old
pine dresser for underwear, muttering, "Hellfire and dam-
nation! All I wanted was a shower. After a two-hundred-
mile drive with a screaming young'un was that too much to
ask?"

Suddenly unsure of this new stranger, the little girl's
mouth quivered. Latching plump baby fingers into Roni's
curls, she buried her face in the disheveled mass and re-
newed her howls. Awkwardly, Roni patted the infant's back

while a lump of empathy thickened her throat. She felt as adrift and isolated and scared as the baby, but she had to know one thing.

"Is she yours?"

The rustle of denim and the rasp of a zipper accompanied Sam's deep voice. "Thought I could handle one night on my own. How the hell was I supposed to know—"

"Sam!" Pivoting on her boot heel, Roni held the child protectively against her heart and glared at him. "Is she yours?"

"What?" The sharpness of her voice froze him in the process of snapping his jeans, and he frowned, puzzled. Then his blue eyes widened. "Hell, no! I mean, well—yes, I guess you could say that."

"Make up your mind!" The baby's wails fired Roni's indignation. "I never thought you were the kind of man to cat around with no thought to the consequences, Sam Preston. Honestly, how could you be so irresponsible?"

A deep flush crept up beneath Sam's tan, starting at his bronzed nipples and racing all the way to his earlobes. He snapped his jeans, his square jaw working. "Don't you go flying off the handle at me, Veronica Jean! She's not mine."

Roni's hands tightened reflexively around the sobbing baby as if to defend her against his callous repudiation. "She has your eyes," she accused hotly. "And you just said—"

"My cousin Roy from Abilene—the one who was killed last year on the oil rig—Jessie's his daughter."

An instantaneous spurt of disgraceful relief filled Roni, quickly masked by total confusion. "Then what, why—?"

"Jessie's mother, Alicia, had a toxic reaction to some medication last week. She went into shock, and there was nothing they could do."

Roni stared at him in blank horror, the baby's cries filling her ears. "She... she's dead?"

At his curt nod, Roni sat down heavily on the side of the unmade king-size bed. Sympathy welled within her, and she instinctively rocked her body in time with little Jessie's hiccuping breaths. "Oh, Sam, I'm so sorry!"

His expression softened into lines of weary sadness, and he cupped his large palm over the infant's soft burgundy-red curls in an attitude of tender protectiveness. "I made the arrangements. The funeral was Saturday. The neighbors were keeping Jessie, but there's no other family except me, so I... well, I'm taking her."

"Oh, Sam!"

His wide mouth tightened with belligerence. "What the hell else was I supposed to do?"

"Oh, Sam, you lunkhead! You misunderstand me." Roni caught his hand. "Of course you have to take her. I wouldn't have expected less."

He hesitated, then sat down beside Roni and gave her fingers a grateful squeeze. "You don't think I'm addled?"

"Hardly. We've been friends since before I could walk, and if there's one thing I know, it's that Sam Preston can be counted on to do the right thing."

"My judgment might be a bit cloudy right now." He pinched the bridge of his nose, lines of fatigue making him look much older than his thirty-seven years. For the first time Roni saw how tired he really was. "It's been a hell of a week."

"I can imagine." Roni stroked Jessie's damp forehead, crooning. "Poor little thing. Poor Jessie. And poor Sam."

"I'm okay."

"Remember who you're talking to, buckaroo?" Roni's coffee-brown eyes were gentle. "You may come across tough as old rawhide to the rest of the world, but I know your heart is made of molasses taffy. So you want to be a father, do you?"

His mouth twisted. "Seems I got no choice. But I swear I had no idea you had to be Dr. Spock, Mother Teresa and an octopus all rolled together to take care of one little baby girl! And if I don't get out there first thing in the morning and help Angel load those bulls for the Ferguson shipment, the Lazy Diamond is really going to be up the creek."

Roni nodded, fully aware that the life on a working ranch never ceased. Angel Morales, Sam's cow boss, ran the day-to-day care of the herds. Angel gave the cowboys who lived in the handful of cottages and trailer homes scattered around the Lazy Diamond their daily riding orders while his wife, Maria, cooked for the hands, but it was Sam who had to meet the demands of owner, general manager and ranch foreman every day.

Sam ran a hand through his damp hair and turned pleading eyes to Roni. "I'm telling you, Curly, I'm frazzled. You gotta help me!"

"Me? In case you forgot, I don't know any more about babies than you do."

Roni couldn't prevent a grimace at the memory of her on-again, off-again relationship with filmmaker Jackson Dial. It had been an eight-year, coast-to-coast stint in self-inflicted misery, which she'd finally put to an end two years earlier when she'd returned to her little hometown of Flat Fork to lick her wounds and pursue her career as a free-lance illustrator. Thanks to Jackson's no-commitment policy, she was single, childless and well on her way to becoming an old maid. Although Sam had listened to her cry in her beer about all of that on innumerable occasions, apparently desperation had made him forget she was as limited in the parental experience department as he was.

"Come on, Curly," Sam begged. "You've got to know something—you're a woman!"

Roni snorted. "Glad you finally noticed."

"Aw, hell, you know what I mean." Sam shoved fingers through his hair again and scrubbed a palm down his beard-stubbled face.

"I know you're a chauvinist at heart." Roni couldn't hide a wry smile at his obvious distress. Then she took pity on him. "Well, to start with, she's soaking wet."

"What—again?"

Roni shifted the baby, now snubbing sibilantly, and plucked at her own sodden shirt. "And she's done a fair job of drenching me, too."

"Damn," he groaned, reaching for the child. "I'm sorry, Curly."

"Take it easy, cowboy. No use both of us getting wet. Find me a diaper and a dry shirt or something for her, will you?"

Nodding, Sam reached for a bulging diaper bag decorated with yellow ducks while Roni laid Jessie on the bed. Worn-out from crying, too tired to even crawl, the baby flailed halfheartedly, her fingers still tangled in Roni's whiskey-colored locks.

But when Roni attempted to detach Jessie's hold, the child would have none of it, whimpering pitifully. It occurred to Roni that Jessie's mother must have had long hair, and the baby was finding some comfort in the familiar scent and texture. Her heart melted.

"All right, sweetie, you can hold on." Ignoring the discomfort of pulled hair, Roni began stripping off the soaked gown and diaper, still talking softly. "Aunt Roni's going to fix you up."

"Here." Sam tossed a clean sleeper on the bed and thrust a disposable diaper at her. "Maybe you can figure out how to keep the damn thing on."

"I've changed Krystal's youngest a time or two," she admitted. Krystal Harrison was another longtime friend from high school. She and her husband, Bud, and their three little boys had welcomed Roni back to Flat Fork with open arms.

"I knew you'd been holding out on me," Sam muttered. He watched uncertainly as Roni smoothed the diaper's adhesive tabs into place. "Think she's hungry again?"

"Tired mostly, but a bottle of something might help soothe her."

Sam nodded again. "Okay. Be right back."

By the time Roni pulled the dry sleeper onto Jessie's sturdy little body, Sam had returned with a plastic baby bottle.

"It's juice. Apple, I think. Mrs. Newton, the lady who was keeping Jessie, fixed a bunch of bottles and stuff to tide me over."

"That was thoughtful of her."

"Yeah. She and her husband have five kids of their own. It tore them up about Alicia, and they're real attached to Jessie. Told me they'd keep her as long as I needed, but they aren't well-off, and I couldn't let Jessie be a burden on them. Besides, I felt it was important to get her settled here as soon as possible."

Seating herself in an old platform rocker whose threadbare upholstery had seen better days, Roni offered the baby the juice. Jessie latched on to the nipple with a sigh, and her fine lashes drifted down against her plump cheeks, one hand still tightly clutching Roni's hair. Roni set the rocker in motion, then looked up at the tall man watching her.

"Seriously, Sam, what do you mean to do? Taking on a baby is a pretty tall order for a bachelor."

Jamming his hands into his front pockets, he bowed his head and stared at the floor a long moment. Roni saw his Adam's apple bob revealingly. "When Roy died, I promised Alicia I'd always look out for her and the baby. I promised."

At that simple, yet all-encompassing and life-changing statement, Roni's heart turned over with both admiration and compassion. Simultaneously, a part of her couldn't help but notice his casual, all-male stance. The way his lean hip cocked, stretching the denim of his jeans provocatively, might have made a more susceptible female's libido jump into high gear. The thing about Sam was that he truly didn't understand how potent he could be to the opposite sex. It was one of his more endearing qualities.

He looked up. "I'll hire a housekeeper, I guess, though where I'll get the extra money right now I don't know. Maybe if I can beat Travis King out of that Wichita Rodeo contract..."

He trailed off at the mention of his rival. There was bad blood between them. Though Sam never spoke of it, Roni knew it was due to King's involvement in the auto accident that had taken Sam's brother's life more than a decade earlier. Now he shook his head, as if to clear it of painful memories, continuing with the subject at hand.

"And then there's baby-sitters and day care. Other people do it. I can, too."

Jessie had fallen asleep at last, and Roni set the unfinished juice bottle aside. When she transferred the sleeping infant to her shoulder, Jessie's tiny sigh of contentment tugged at her heartstrings in a way that was as powerful as it was unexpected. Stroking the baby's curls and inhaling the sweet scent of her skin evoked maternal instincts Roni hadn't even been aware she possessed.

"Being a parent takes more than just meeting a child's physical needs, Sam," she said softly.

"I know that. But the little kid's already been through more hell than most people face in a lifetime! Besides, I can't turn my back on blood kin. I always regretted that Shelly and I didn't have a kid or two. Well, Jessie needs a family, so I figure God's giving me a second chance to be a father."

His words made Roni swallow hard with sudden emotion, part genuine admiration for his determination and willingness to take on such a commitment, part pure envy that he should have such a rare opportunity to explore the trials and joys of family love. To cover an unexpected prickle of tears, Roni glanced down at the sleeping child. "Have you got a bed made for her?"

Sam pulled his hands free of his pockets and gestured toward the hall. "I put her playpen in my old room."

Nodding, her composure restored, Roni rose carefully and followed him into the cluttered bedroom next door. The small lamp on the bedside table illuminated wall-hung bookshelves filled with high school athletic and rodeo trophies won by Sam and his brother. Sam's parents had never really recovered from Kenny's death. They were gone now, too, and apparently not even Shelly's brief occupancy had made an impact on this old room. Now an ancient, but still-prized saddle sat on the desk and Sam's rodeo and cattle breeding journals lay strewn on the twin bed and floor.

Roni laid the baby in the playpen, covered her with a crocheted blanket, then stood back. "She's a beautiful child, Sam."

Sam placed an arm around Roni's shoulder in a familiar, companionable gesture. The heat of his body and the fresh scent of soap enveloped her as they gazed down at the sleeping infant.

"Yeah, she's a heartbreaker, all right, and I'll admit I'm smitten. I want to do what's right for her, Curly."

"I know you will." Twisting the knob on the lamp, she led him from the room, leaving the door cracked behind them. Pausing in the hall, she gave him a mock-serious look. "You're going to have to do something about that decor, you know. Little girls need frills and lace, bonnets and patent-leather shoes, baby dolls and kittens."

"As I recall, Miss Tomboy, you never did." Now that things were back under control—at least for the moment—Sam shot her a glance sparked with a glimmer of his usual laid-back mischief and gave a lock of her unruly hair a teasing tug. "Blue jeans and horses and hauling it around hell-bent-for-leather after the rest of us boys was the only thing that ever interested you coming up."

"Could I help it if I was the only girl in a ten-mile radius? Besides, there's an exception to every rule." Despite their close friendship, there was a thing or two Sam Preston didn't know about her and her intimate likes and dislikes. Inwardly amused, she made her tone mild. "And you might be surprised what catches a girl's fancy."

"I know I've got a lot to learn."

"Oh, yes, indeed." Roni counted items off on her fingers. "Ballet lessons, hair bows, kissing scratched knees, wiping tears, not to mention those talks when she hits puberty, buying her first bra and warning her about what boys are really after—"

"Good God."

The dismay on Sam's face was so comical, Roni laughed aloud. Impulsively, she laid a hand on his bare shoulder and came up on tiptoe to kiss his cheek. "You're a good man, Sam Preston, and I'm a fiend to tease you when you're so exhausted. I'll go, but I'll check on you first thing in the morning, okay? Maybe Krystal can recommend some names for the housekeeper's position.''

''Uh, Curly?''

''Yeah?''

''You want a cup of coffee or something? Or how about a beer?''

Roni frowned. ''Do you know what time it is?''

''We could turn on the late show and shoot the breeze for a while. Anything happen down at Rosie's I should know about?''

''I'll tell you tomorrow. I'm going home to bed.''

''Uh . . . do you have to?''

Brown eyes narrowed, Roni gave Sam a searching look. Could what she spied darting behind his brilliant blue gaze be...fear? Not Sam Preston, the man who could coolly face down a maddened Brahma bull and never bat an eyelash. Not strong, silent Sam, the bulwark of the community, the man who'd taken his wife's walking out on him because she couldn't stand small-town life with such quiet dignity, he'd earned the admiration of the whole county.

Roni's lips quirked, and her respect for little Jessie's feminine wiles went up several notches. Was that really big, bad Sam Preston quaking in his bare size twelves at the thought of being left at the mercy of one tiny little girl?

''You don't really want to watch the late show, do you?'' she asked, holding back her laughter with difficulty.

''Have a little pity, will you, Curly?'' His lean cheeks heated with consternation. ''What if I don't hear Jessie cry? You know what a hard sleeper I am. And what if she gets sick during the night? I'd just have to call you again.''

Inspecting her paint-stained nails, Roni gave an airy reply. ''I could always take my phone off the hook.''

Sam's expression turned sour. "You're going to make me beg, aren't you?"

She did laugh then. "No, I think I'll reserve that pleasure for when you're really desperate."

"Then you'll stay? Just for tonight? So I can find my sea legs?"

Having already made an emotional connection with Jessie, Roni's answer was a foregone conclusion, but she wouldn't let Sam off that hook that easily. "Well ... if it'll make you feel better."

"Oh, it will." Relief made his deep voice husky. "You don't know."

"I can guess." She chuckled. "I'll even take the bed in her room. There's one condition, though."

"Anything." At her devilish look, he added hastily, "Within reason."

"You know, Sam," she mused, running a goading finger down his hair-dusted breastbone, "another woman might try to take advantage of this situation. Having you over a barrel could be very ... profitable."

He caught her wrist, shaking his head in warning, his own grin twitching the corners of his mouth as the familiar give-and-take of their usual teasing reasserted itself.

"If you play with fire, lady, you might get burned. So spit it out. You want a trade? Okay, I'll pick up the tab at Rosie's for a month. How's that?"

"Penny ante," she scoffed. "Up the stakes a little, you cheapskate."

"I'll see that the fence down on the south boundary line between our places gets patched."

"You were going to do that anyway."

He shook her arm gently, growling, "So what do you want?"

"Diablo."

Thunderstruck, Sam stared, his sandy eyebrows lifting in surprise. "Hell, I'm not going to give you my prize stallion!"

"I just want to ride him."

"Uh-uh. No way. He'll break your neck."

"I ride as well as you do!" she protested, tugging free of his grasp. "Well, almost."

"Look, Curly, I value your hide too much to risk it atop that devil." Sam perched his fists on his lean hips and glowered down at her. "And don't tell me all those years in New York art school and then working out in L.A. didn't take the edge off your skills, because I won't buy it. You've got to have a little common sense about such things."

"Any second now," she warned darkly, "I'm liable to burst out in a chorus of 'Anything You Can Do, I Can Do Better.'"

"Curly, I swear—"

She laughed suddenly at his exasperation. "Relax, Sam, I won't press you if you feel that strongly, but one of these days, me and Diablo . . ." She winked at him. "Until then, I'll just have to make my own fun getting you riled up."

"And one of these days I'm going to throttle you."

"No, you won't," she retorted, smug. "Who else'll babysit for you for free? You're going to have to think about these things now."

"You may have a point." He stifled a yawn.

"Go to bed, Sam," she said kindly. "I know where you keep your linens, and I can help myself. Remember, little children have a tendency to get up with the sun."

"I don't need a second invitation. Good night." He turned toward his room.

Roni tugged at her damp shirt and wrinkled her nose. "Have you got something I can sleep in?"

"In the bathroom cupboard. Watch out for that hot water spigot. It's loose and cantankerous."

"I remember."

"And, Roni?"

She paused at the bathroom door. A peculiar little stirring fluttered in her chest at both the solemnity and the affection she saw in his dark blue eyes. "Yes, Sam?"

"Thanks."

Smiling, Roni shrugged. "Hey, what are best friends for?"


There was a newborn calf bawling outside, and sooner or later Sam was going to have to get up and see to it. He pulled his pillow over his ears and groaned.

*But not yet, damn you.*

One eye flew open. The angle of the morning sun falling through his bedroom window was a lot higher than it should have been. And there was something he ought to remember...*Jessie!*

Sam jackknifed out of bed. He was leaning over the empty playpen in the next room before the sleep cleared from his groggy brain, and for an awful moment of panic and guilt he thought he'd misplaced her. Then he heard baby gurgles and Roni's soft laughter floating from the direction of the kitchen.

He took only a second to pull on jeans, then came up short in the doorway of the large country kitchen. Stretched out on the rag rug underneath the trestle table was a pair of long, long feminine legs and a shapely behind. She was decent only by the length of a man's shirttail.

"Peekaboo, Jessie. Where's Jessie?"

Roni peered around a chair leg at the little girl, who clapped and bounced on her diaper-clad bottom in delight at the game, then took off scrambling on all fours around the opposite side of the table. Roni came to her knees, too, stalking her prey with a mock ferocity that made the child squeal—just like a calf stuck in a fence, Sam thought.

Leaning his shoulder against the door frame, he grinned, remembering times past when he and Kenny and Roni had played much the same kind of game in this very kitchen, building imaginary forts and corrals in and among the chair rungs, fighting off savage Indians and rustlers with their trusty six-guns. Of course, at that time none of them had sported anything like the provocative candy-pink lace he glimpsed peeking from beneath the hem of the old white dress shirt Roni had slept in.

After an instant's honest masculine appreciation, he dragged his gaze reluctantly to a more respectful perusal of the rich brown sleep-tousled curls spilling down the middle of her back. Though she liked to keep her mop ruthlessly clipped back and tidy these days, it was still more than clear why she'd earned her nickname. He'd teased her unmercifully about her mane one summer—at least until she'd bloodied his nose with an uppercut that had laid him out flat and taught him a valuable lesson about women.

Chuckling at the memory, he watched Roni creep after Jessie, poking her way through a litter of oat cereal "O's" and discarded paper napkins. It was an amazement and a miracle to him that his childhood playmate was still such an important part of his life. He was selfishly glad she'd finally had the good sense to break things off with that no-good jet-setting scoundrel she'd been involved with and come home to Flat Fork where she belonged.

The mess he'd made with Shelly had made him gun-shy when it came to matters of the heart, and if it hadn't been for Roni Daniels bullying him back into life, he surely would have become a hermit. Instead, over their Friday-night beers at Rosie's, she'd cajoled him and talked him into reentering life while nursing her own bruised heart.

Sam didn't know what he would have done without her, and now, here she was again, pitching in like the true pal she was, giving him her unequivocal support to a decision that no doubt half the county would consider as cracked as the Liberty Bell.

And, on top of that, she'd taken the early shift.

"Morning, you two."

Jessie's russet curls bobbed at the sound of Sam's sleep-husky voice, and her blue eyes widened in recognition. Forgetting the game, she scrambled madly across the floor toward him with a squeal. "Da!"

She was irresistible. Sam bent and scooped the tyke into his arms as Roni sat back on her heels and eyed the duo.

"So what am I now, chopped liver?" she mock complained.

Sam grinned. "Sorry, Curly. Can I help it if women of all ages find me fascinating?"

Roni gave an indelicate snort. "You wish, cowboy."

Hauling herself to her feet, she flicked her dark hair over her shoulders and straightened the oversize shirt. From the stains on the front, Jessie's first breakfast in her new home had been a challenging experience. Ocher and peach-colored splatters dotted the fabric, but not quite enough to obscure the faint dark shadows of Roni's nipples showing beneath the white cotton.

Sam frowned to himself. Now why had he noticed that? Roni was his buddy, like the sister he never had. Still, he wouldn't have been much of a man not to appreciate the way the crests of her full bosom poked against...

"Ready for a taste?" Roni sashayed to the counter and lifted a cup in an invitation that slid in under Sam's defenses and landed hot in his belly.

*Hell, yes! He'd like to taste those impudent buds, lave
them with his tongue right through the thin cotton until the
fabric was wet and transparent and so was...*

Roni was frowning at his lack of response. "Sam? Your
coffee?"

Savagely, Sam reigned in his meandering thoughts. Jeez,
he'd been without female companionship way too long
when he started fantasizing about Curly! The last thing he
wanted was to spoil their friendship with inappropriate
lasciviousness.

"Uh, yeah. Thanks." He shifted the chortling baby to
the opposite shoulder and shook his groggy head. Yeah,
that was it. He was still sleep-muddled. "You should have
gotten me up sooner."

She passed him a mug of steaming coffee, shrugging.
"You obviously needed the rest. And Jessie and I have been
getting acquainted. She's quite a charmer."

As if in response, the little girl nestled her cheek in the
hollow of Sam's collarbone and batted her long eyelashes
at him in a look that was pure coquettishness. "Da?"

Sam's laugh was helpless. "I'm a goner, as you can see."

"Yes, indeed." Roni cupped her hands around her own
mug and gazed at him over the rim, her brown eyes serious. "Sure you know what you're getting into?"

"No." The twist of his mouth was wry. "But I'm in over
my head, and it's too late now."

"Then I'll help you all I can," she said simply.

Her unqualified generosity produced a suspicious thick-
ness in his throat. "Thanks, Curly. I—I don't quite know
what to say."

"Just tell me what you want for breakfast, because I
think that's Angel's old truck I hear coming down the lane,
and you've got some bulls to see to."

"Damn! He's here already? I'm running later than I thought." He took a step toward the bedroom, hesitated as he realized he still held Jessie, then passed her off to Roni with an apologetic look. "Sorry. Can you stay a bit? Just until we get the livestock loaded."

"Relax, Sam. Everything's under control." Roni tickled the baby's chin and was rewarded with a giggle. "You see to those bulls, and I'll give Krystal a call about prospective housekeepers."

He shoved a hand through his hair and blew out a breath. "That would be a big help."

"Don't worry. I'm sure Krystal and I will have something worked out by suppertime." Roni bounced the baby on her hip, her smile complacent. "After all, Jessie's a doll. How hard could it be?"

# Two

"So what's wrong with *this* one?"

"Her nose is too long."

"You've got to be kidding." Sam flung his pencil down on a list of crossed-out names and glared in exasperation at Roni over the charred crusts of their frozen pizza lunch.

"Well, figuratively speaking, anyway," she muttered, folding one of Jessie's gowns and placing it in a plastic laundry basket with the rest of the baby's clean things. "Mrs. Hawkins is the worst gossip in town. She'll spend all of her time talking on the phone instead of looking after Jessie."

"Well, what about Laurie Taylor?"

"She's barely out of high school. Do you want all her randy boyfriends hanging around all the time?"

Sam reared back in his chair, eyeing Roni with a degree of belligerence. In her paint-spattered T-shirt, cutoffs and bare feet, she didn't look much older than a teenager herself. And when she was in one of her ornery moods—as now—Sam was of the opinion that what she really needed was a darned good spanking. "You suggest someone then."

"Agnes Phillips," she said promptly.

"What?" His chair legs hit the floor with a smack. "She's so old, she creaks when she walks—or rather, shuffles." Sam gestured to where Jessie sat on the kitchen floor, babbling to herself and playing with an assortment of pots and wooden spoons. "She couldn't keep up with the little trickster here for ten seconds."

Roni merely shrugged. "Then you'll just have to keep looking, won't you?"

Sam scowled, rubbed his palms down his sweat-stained jeans and began to roll up the cuffs of his long-sleeved chambray work shirt with every evidence of severe irritation. Punching cows since dawn hadn't done much for his mood, and Roni's stubbornness wasn't helping.

"We've been interviewing for three days now, Curly. We're no closer to hiring anyone than when we started, and the county welfare worker is due out here at three to see how everything's going. What am I going to tell her?"

"That you're still interviewing applicants. No one expects miracles in just a few short days."

He grimaced sourly. "Yeah, but at the rate we're going, we'll run out of Flat Fork residents before I find a suitable housekeeper."

Roni bristled. "I can't help it that you're so darned picky."

"Me? You rejected the most promising candidates out of hand." Sam ticked off names on the list. "Davina Hodge is too strict. Mrs. Rambles is too wishy-washy. Cloretha Glover has bad breath."

"Well, you can't settle for just anyone as Jessie's primary caretaker. This decision is too important to rush."

Finished with her chore, she plopped the laundry basket down beside the door. "Besides, I told you my deadline for the *Artbeat* cover illustration isn't for three weeks, so I don't mind helping out."

"But you can't camp out here indefinitely," he argued.

Her lips twisted with wry humor. "I know I'm not much of a cook, but I didn't realize I'd worn out my welcome already."

"Hey, even incinerated pizza tastes good after a morning vaccinating calves—" He saw her expression and added hastily, "Not that I'm complaining. I appreciate all you're doing."

"Then what's the problem?"

"Well, uh—" He shifted uncomfortably. "Aw, hell, Curly! What're folks liable to say, seeing as how you've practically moved in with me?"

"Oh, for crying out loud!" She rolled her eyes in disgust. "They'll say that I'm just helping out a buddy until he gets this daddy thing under control. Since you're so busy catching up on the work that accumulated while you were away, it's simply more convenient for me to sleep here, and easier on Jessie, too."

"I just don't want you to catch any guff—"

"The only thing I'm liable to catch is a backache from that lumpy twin bed in Jessie's room. And maybe ptomaine from all the prepared food we've had out of your freezer. Don't cowboys ever eat salad or fresh vegetables?"

"Not if we can help it." Her dismissal of his concern and return to her normal teasing made him relax, and his lips twitched. "But maybe I could force some down if it's accompanied by a nice, thick T-bone steak."

Her brown eyes lit up. "You offering to grill them?"

"Yup."

"You've got yourself a deal."

On the floor, Jessie had abandoned her spoons and sat rubbing her eyes and fretting softly. Scooping up the baby, Roni cuddled her close. Jessie immediately stuck her thumb in her mouth and buried her other fist into Roni's hair in what was fast becoming a familiar habit. While the child seemed to be settling in, she alternated periods of normal behavior with listlessness or extreme irritability—a sure sign that she was grieving for her missing mother. And all the more reason to provide a loving and dependable daily caretaker as soon as possible, Sam thought.

"She's tired," Roni said.

"Want me to rock her?"

Roni dropped a kiss on the baby's forehead. "No, I'll do it. But since you've got to hang around to meet the caseworker, I'm going to run home for a change of clothes while she's napping."

"Sure. Take as much time as you need." Sam nodded, guilty that his new status as dad was disrupting Roni's routine. Despite her protests to the contrary, he knew that her career was booming and that her schedule was fairly tight. If he didn't hire someone soon, Roni's work would suffer and then he'd *really* be wallowing in the guilt.

Not for the first time, he wondered if he'd made the right decision. A flock of butterflies seemed to have taken up permanent residence in his belly at the enormity of what he was doing. But he'd promised Alicia he'd take care of her daughter, and he was a man of his word.

"I won't be long," Roni said, settling the tired baby against her shoulder. "I'll pick up the dinner fixings and give Krystal a holler, too. Maybe she can think of someone else who might be interested in the housekeeper's position."

Picking up the list again, Sam stared at it gloomily. "And anyone whose name isn't Mary Poppins need not apply."

Laughing at his morose expression, she turned and headed for Jessie's room. "Don't worry, Sam. I'm sure the perfect solution is right under our noses. It's simply a matter of finding it."

Two and a half hours later, Roni pulled her Jeep into Krystal Harrison's sunny driveway. She felt rather breathless after her quick trip home. Since her widowed mother, Carolyn, had married hardware store owner Jinks Robinson and moved to Austin, Roni had the tiny Daniels homestead to herself, but today the house had seemed more silent and solitary than usual.

She'd lingered only long enough to check her mail and pick up clean clothes, then headed to the tiny Flat Fork post office to express a piece of advertising art that should have gone off two days earlier. She followed a stop by the library to pick up the latest child development and parenting guides with a visit to the Winn-Dixie for groceries. One more stop to pick Krystal's brain for potential housekeepers, and then she could be on her way back to Sam's place. Roni anxiously hoped that he'd managed to hold down the fort without her.

A trio of towheaded wild Indians erupted from the carport of the single-story brick ranch house that matched its neighbors in this small, tree-lined subdivision.

"Aunt Roni!"

"Hey, Mom. Aunt Roni's here!"

"Did ya bring us anything?"

Roni reached for the packs of sugarless bubble gum Krystal's boys had come to expect, then hastily tucked the hem of a scarlet silk-and-lace teddy back out of sight in her tote bag. No use giving the little rascals any embarrassing fodder for their question mill. After all, if a gal had a secret hankering for flimsy underthings, it was nobody's business but her own.

In a town where the pace of life was slow and casual, Roni didn't have much call for the slinky, sexy dresses she'd worn when she'd been continually on Jackson Dial's arm. But just because her working attire was jeans and T-shirts, and her going-out attire was *clean* jeans and a T-shirt, didn't mean she'd lost her love of feminine frills altogether. In a small, churchgoing town like Flat Fork, however, it was better to keep one's scandalous predilections private.

"Hello, boys. Yes, here you go." Stepping out of the Jeep, Roni passed out gum to Kevin, Kelly and Karl amid a profusion of thanks. "Where's your mother?"

"In the backyard," Kelly replied. "She says to come on back."

Roni grinned and ruffled the third grader's fair bangs. "Thanks."

"You gonna come watch me play tee-ball Saturday?" four-year-old Karl demanded.

"I'm sure going to try, partner." Roni walked through the carport into the spacious backyard littered with an assortment of balls, bats and toy trucks. Krystal, a petite blonde with a short wedge haircut, hailed her from a lounge chair on the brick patio.

"You're just in time for something cool," she said, pouring a tall glass of ice tea from a plastic pitcher on a nearby snack table. "It's the lull before the suppertime, homework and 'oh-Mom-do-I-have-to-go-to-bed-now' storm."

"Sounds good." Roni flung herself down in a matching chair, smiling. Though she might complain about it, Krystal's day-to-day family life was bursting with energy and her home full of love—something that Roni thought any woman would envy.

"I can't stay but a minute," she said. "I'm already much later than I thought I'd be, and Sam's just about helpless when Jessie gets into her evening snit."

Krystal handed the glass to Roni. "Seems to me he'd better learn to handle it if he means to keep her."

"Oh, he does! You should just see how he melts when she bats her baby blues at him. It's the cutest thing you ever saw."

"Who?" Krystal smirked. "Jessie or Sam?"

Roni laughed and sipped her tea. "Well, both of them, I guess. She's got a temper to match those red curls, but she's a sweetheart. I swear she's already calling Sam 'Da-Da.' He's just wild to find a housekeeper so she can have some sort of routine, but so far, no luck at all."

"None of the ladies I suggested were interested?" Krystal asked incredulously.

Roni shook her head. "Well, some of them were interested, but Sam's so hard to please." She explained who had been interviewed and the various reasons they'd been found unsuitable. "You don't know of anyone else, do you?"

Frowning, Krystal hesitated. "I'll have to think about it. In the meantime, I suppose Sam could enroll Jessie in Pharis Fitzgerald's Mother Goose Day Care."

"What? Drag that baby out of her bed at the crack of dawn every morning and leave her with a bunch of strangers until dusk? Out of the question!" Roni blushed at her own vehemence. "I mean, I'm sure Sam wants to keep her at home. She's been through so many changes, you see, and she gets upset easily—"

"Sounds to me as though you don't *want* to find someone to hire."

"That's ridiculous." Roni brushed her curls out of her hot face. "I simply want Sam to find the best person for the job."

"So you can get on with your highly exciting life, right?" Krystal nodded sagely. "You can't fool me, Roni Daniels. You're having a whale of a time mothering that baby."

Roni laughed, unable to deny the accusation. "Can I help it if I'm a pushover for redheaded cherubs?"

"Got it that bad, huh? So tell me, how's it really going? Everyone in this town is mighty interested in what's happening with that baby... and you."

"Me?" Roni blinked. "Why me?"

Krystal gave her friend a disgusted look. "You must be the only female in this town immune to Sam Preston's sex appeal. Do I have to draw you a picture? You, plus Sam, plus one adorable orphan, emotions running high, close proximity—"

"Sheesh, Krystal, not you, too!" Roni took a long pull of her ice tea. "I'm just being a good neighbor."

"And you never noticed that Sam Preston is one handsome hunk of raw masculinity?"

Roni fought back a mental flash of Sam clad only in a towel, and said loftily, "I admire Sam for a lot of reasons. He's my best friend, after all."

"Let me tell you, there are plenty of single ladies in this town who'd give their right arms to be in your shoes—especially Nadine Scott."

Roni grimaced. Nadine was the new hospital administrator who'd gone out with Sam a couple of times. "Well, she can stop holding her breath. There's nothing happening between her and Sam."

"How do you know?"

"He told me. Said she's too aggressive and wears too much makeup. I happen to agree."

Krystal laughed and crossed her ankles on the lounger. "So that's what you two talk about every Friday night. You dissect each other's dates."

"Not always. Well, sometimes," Roni admitted grudgingly. "Sam warned me Tully Carson was a card-carrying chauvinist. Boy, was he right."

"The way the two of you rip each other's suitors to shreds, it's a wonder you have any social life at all. And Sam's going to need one now more than ever."

"What do you mean?"

"While everyone applauds his good intentions regarding little Jessie, that baby's going to need a mother. But the way things are, no eligible single gal can get to Sam because she has to go through you."

Totally taken aback, Roni could only stare. "I—I never thought of that."

"You have to admit that Sam's one of the few genuinely nice men left around here."

"Of course he is."

"Not like Jackson."

Roni's lips twisted. "Certainly not like Jackson Dial."

Krystal searched her friend's expression. "You're really over him, aren't you?"

"After two years, the hurt fades. I could kick myself for sticking it out so long, hoping—" She shook her head.

"He's got a new movie out, I see."

"Yes, I know. *Apache Tears.* I actually did some of the preliminary sketches for the art direction. For free, of course. That's Jackson's style." Shaking off the feeling of failure that remembering their relationship always evoked, she set down her glass and rose. "I've got to run. Call me if you think of anyone else who might want the housekeeper's position, okay?"

Minutes later Roni sped down the two-lane blacktop toward the Lazy Diamond, chewing her lip in worry. Could Krystal be right? Had she been doing Sam a disservice by monopolizing his time, to the detriment of any other relationship he might develop? Sam was such a decent man, he deserved a woman who would adore him, someone unlike Shelly, who'd appreciate his strong ties to the land and the little community he called home.

Forcing herself to look at the situation with brutal honesty, Roni had to admit that she'd grown to depend on Sam's steadfastness, his lazy humor, the easy, accepting friendship. Since her return, he'd been her sounding board and her shield against loneliness. Now the realization that in her need she'd been depriving him of the chance to find someone special filled her with guilty remorse.

Krystal was absolutely on target. Sam needed a wife and a mother for Jessie, but he was unlikely to find one with Roni in the picture. If she really loved Sam as a friend, then the most generous thing she could do would be to step back so that nature could take its course—even if Sam ended up with someone like Nadine Scott. The image made her lips twist in distaste.

Swallowing hard, Roni pushed the sensation aside. Whatever happened, Sam had to be free to make his own choices. Just as soon as they settled the housekeeper situation, she'd have to start disconnecting herself from her dependency on Sam—for his own good. It was the right thing to do. So why, then, did the thought weigh so heavily on her heart?

Roni was still struggling with this quandary when she parked the Jeep at the ranch house. Juggling two brown paper bags of groceries, she started up the porch steps, only to be met by the sound of Jessie's wails coming from the rear of the house.

She rushed to set her burdens down on the kitchen table, calling out as she went. "Sam, I'm back. What's the matter with Jessie?"

There was no answer but the baby's continued sobbing, and alarm raced down Roni's backbone. She hurried to Jessie's room, appalled to find her in her playpen, red-faced, alone and wailing as if her heart were broken.

"Oh, honey!" Roni's heart tightened at the upsetting sight, and her anger blossomed. Where the devil was Sam? How could he have left the child all alone? Lifting Jessie into her arms, she tried to calm the baby. "Hush, Jessie. Roni's here. It's all right."

The tiny girl clutched at Roni's hair, arched her back and howled in earnest, giant crocodile tears streaming down her flushed cheeks.

"Come on now, sweetie," Roni said.

A quick check found Jessie's diaper dry, and an almost-full bottle in the corner of the playpen proved it wasn't hunger that fueled the baby's ire. Noticing the child's hot cheeks and sweaty neck, Roni carried her to the bathroom for a cooling cloth. But the damp washcloth only infuriated the child even further, and she kicked and squirmed and screamed in a pure tantrum of ill-tempered misery.

Feeling helpless in the face of such fury, her own frustration spilling over, Roni glanced out the bathroom window and caught a glimpse of Sam engaged in some task down by Diablo's paddock. Appalled, her own fury ignited, due in part to her inadequacy at dealing with Jessie's squalling, and in part to her incredulity at Sam's callousness and utter carelessness. Still holding the struggling baby, she stormed outside.

Sam heard her coming and laid the cinch straps he'd been mending across the top rail of the paddock. Even Diablo, Sam's ebony stallion, raised his elegant head from the hay bale he'd been investigating and pricked his ears toward the ruckus.

Pushing his straw cowboy hat to the back of his head, Sam frowned wearily and demanded, "Why did you pick her up?"

Roni stared. "What? She's screaming at the top of her lungs! Are you out of your ever-loving mind?"

Sam winced at Jessie's ear-piercing wails. "She's been at it all afternoon. Finally figured she'd have to cry it out."

"How could you?" Roni railed, struggling to hold the flailing child. "You don't leave a kid alone like that. What if she's sick? Or hungry? Or—"

"Dammit, Curly, don't you think I've got sense enough to think of all that?" Sam's dark glower was mute evidence that he was near the end of his own rope. "Little bit started up not ten minutes after you left and squalled the whole time the county caseworker was here. I tried everything, and not a damned thing pleases her."

"That's no excuse, Sam Preston," Roni said, her tone accusing. "You left her!"

"Since all I did just seemed to make whatever it is worse, I thought I'd give her some space. Believe me, I could hear her just fine out here. I'm not a complete dunce."

"No, just a heartless one!" Roni shouted to be heard over Jessie's crying. "You can't treat a baby like...like one of your damn cows. Of all the insensitive, moronic—"

"Curse it, that's enough." Sam's expression was black as thunder, and his jaw thrust out at a militant angle. "You weren't here, and I had to follow my best judgment—which was working just fine until you came along and got her started again."

"I did no such—"

"Don't try to second-guess me, Curly," he interrupted brusquely, jabbing his forefinger at her nose. "When it comes right down to it, she's not your responsibility."

Sam's harsh words landed like a physical slap and took Roni's breath. She stared at him, feeling the color drain from her face. Hot tears prickled behind her lids. With a small cry that was barely audible above Jessie's weeping, Roni turned and stumbled for the house.

"Curly, wait. I didn't mean—"

Choking, Roni didn't pause to hear the rest. Calling herself every kind of idiot, she tried to contain the hurt that bubbled over. The worst of it was that despite the affection and attachment for Jessie already blossoming in her unwary heart, Sam was absolutely right. She had no claim on the redheaded angel who was still making a devilish uproar. No bond of blood or commitment, and certainly no right—best friends or no—to instruct Sam on the upbringing of his new daughter. The knowledge left a bitter taste in her mouth.

"Roni, stop!" Sam caught her from behind just as she reached the back door, his expression stricken. "Oh, God, you're crying. You never cry."

"You'd better take her," Roni said around a knot of tears in her throat. "I—" A sob stole whatever else she meant to say.

Cussing a blue streak, Sam shot a harried glance from side to side, then abruptly dragged Roni, still holding the baby, off the porch and toward his blue Ford pickup. Without further explanation he jerked open the door and thrust her inside. A child's car seat sat buckled in the middle of the seat.

"Here, strap her in," he muttered, then pushed Roni's fumbling hands aside to perform the task on the screaming baby.

"Sam, what—? Please..." Distraught and unnerved, Roni tried to slip out past him, but he caught her, buckled her seat belt much as he'd done Jessie's, then slammed the door.

"Stay put." His mouth was grim as he came around to the driver's side. "We're going for a ride."

"I don't want to go anywhere with you!" Sniffling, Roni wiped her tears on the hem of her knit shirt and tried to glare at him. "What's so all-fired important about taking a ride?"

"Read it somewhere," he muttered, starting the vehicle. "Supposed to be soothing to cranky kids or something." He threw the truck into gear and tore down the dusty drive as if all the demons of hell were after them.

"That's if the baby has colic!" Roni shouted over the engine noise and Jessie's continued bellows of rage.

"What have we got to lose?"

"Fine. Suit yourself." Crossing her arms, Roni stared mulishly out the window and said nothing further.

Nearly thirty miles later, Jessie's screams had turned to soft snores. Sam slowed to a more reasonable pace, made a U-turn and headed back toward the ranch.

"I didn't mean it, you know," he said finally.

Roni clamped down on her bottom lip to hide a betraying trembling, then forced herself to speak honestly. "It's true anyway, and I apologize. I overstepped my place. She's not my responsibility."

"Roni, I'm sorry. I didn't mean that the way it sounded." Sam squinted against the orange globe of the sun resting on the western horizon and ran his free hand down his square jaw. "The way you've pitched in, you've got a right to say whatever you think."

Roni stroked Jessie's plump fist, taking care not to wake the sleeping baby. If Sam was offering an olive branch, she would be foolish not to accept it. "Neither one of us has any experience dealing with a little heifer as stubborn as this one."

"She's put me through the wringer, all right. It makes me wonder..." He fell silent.

Something in the tone of his voice made her glance at him sharply. "What, Sam?"

He sighed, bouncing his fist on the steering wheel. "If I'm doing the right thing. That social worker, Mrs. Veatch, asked some pretty tough questions."

A trickle of fear made Roni's voice querulous. "Like what?"

"Like if I'm ready to be a single parent. If taking Jessie, even with the best of intentions, is right for her."

"What else would it be?" she demanded, her eyes growing wide with a premonition of disaster.

"Selfish." Sam's blue gaze flicked to Roni, then snapped back to the highway. "Am I doing this for myself or for her? Maybe Jessie deserves a real family, with a mother and father, somebody who can offer her something more stable than a cowboy's life."

"What are you saying?" Roni whispered. "You'd put her in a foster home?"

"That was one suggestion. But there are plenty of couples who're dying to adopt. She could have all the advantages...."

"Give her up completely?" Roni couldn't hide her dismay.

"It's not something I'd do lightly. But, dammit, Curly, I just don't know if I'm cut out for this, and Jessie needs two parents."

Rather desperately, Roni said, "You might get married again."

"Old bachelor like me?" Sam grimaced. "Not likely. And I don't exactly have a sterling record in the marriage department anyway."

"That wasn't your fault," she muttered, chagrined anew that her presence might have played a part in his failure to find another partner. And now Jessie could pay the price, as well. "And what about your promise to Alicia?"

A muscle worked in Sam's lean jaw, and his eyes narrowed, picking out the turn to the Lazy Diamond. "I said I'd take care of Jessie. Finding a stable home environment where she can grow up secure and loved is the best way for me to keep that promise."

"You don't have to decide right now, do you?"

Her words were so strangled with tension that Sam glanced sharply at her.

"Do you?" she demanded, feeling brittle.

"No." They'd reached the ranch house, and now he parked the truck and turned on the seat, meeting Roni's anxious gaze across the top of Jessie's car seat. "But I'm going to think on it hard."

Roni slumped with relief, then hid her reaction by releasing Jessie from her harness. The exhausted baby was limp, her cherub's mouth parted in the soft breaths of slumber and she made scarcely a murmur as Roni lifted her free. Sam had come around to the passenger side by this time and helped Roni climb out. His hand was warm on her upper arm, holding her still as he looked down into her face.

"I'm depending on you to help me figure this out, Curly. No matter that I'm already crazy about the kid, I've got to do what's best for her in the long run."

Roni caught a tremulous breath. "I know, Sam."

He gave her arm a brief squeeze that was part thanks, part encouragement, and they went inside. Roni hadn't made it halfway down the hall when the phone rang. The baby on her shoulder jumped, then begin to mewl fretfully. Sam cursed and hurried to the kitchen, catching the receiver up before the next ring. Gratefully, Roni sought out the platform rocker in his bedroom. Rocking and singing softly as daylight fled and the room grew shadowy, she was much relieved when Jessie gave a tired sigh and settled back down.

After a while, Roni heard Sam hang up, and when he appeared in the doorway a moment later, a peculiar expression etched his rugged features. "The Lord works in mysterious ways."

She gave him a curious look. "What? Who was that?"

"Maybe the answer."

Roni's voice was soft, to avoid waking the child she cradled in her arms, but her tone was wry. "Spit it out, Sam. You know your laconic cowboy persona drives me bats."

"About Jessie." He crossed to where Roni sat and swept callused fingers over the tiny girl's russet curls. "That was Mrs. Veatch. She says the Newtons have reconsidered. They're missing Jessie like crazy and want to begin adoption proceedings."

"No." Roni's heart lurched, and her arms tightened involuntarily around the child.

"Curly, we've got to be practical about this."

"Cold-blooded, you mean?" Roni's expression was fierce. "I won't believe it of you, Sam. Tell me you don't care about Jessie. I dare you."

"I'll be damned if I let my emotions cloud what's best for her," he said.

"See? You can't deny it, because you already love her as though she was your own flesh and blood." Gazing down into the sleeping child's rosebud face, Roni felt a wave of emotion pulling her under, forcing her to admit the truth.

She gave a small, breathless cry of surrender. "And so do I."

Sam's expression was suddenly full of worry and concern. He squatted down on his heels beside the rocker so that their eyes were on the same level. "Curly..."

"I want this child. You can't give her away, Sam. I won't let you."

He groaned. "But we've got to think about what's right for Jessie."

"How about what's right for you? For me?" Roni demanded.

Sam threw up his hands. "So what do you want me to do?"

Cheeks pale, Roni hesitated, then met his gaze. "The right thing. Marry me, Sam."

# Three

When Sam was seventeen, he'd been kicked in the head by a half-broken saddle bronc Kenny had dared him to ride. Roni's words produced the same stunning sensation, the impression of falling endlessly until you hit the ground—hard.

"What did you say?" The huskiness of his own voice startled him.

Rosy color flooded Roni's face, but she held his gaze unwaveringly. "I—I think I just proposed, Sam."

"I'm not in the mood for your teasing, Curly."

"I'm dead serious."

Sam rose abruptly. Roni's warm brown eyes seemed huge in her pale face, and he was suddenly struck by how pretty she was, even disheveled with her dark hair curling about her shoulders, and how absolutely right she looked, cradling a baby to her bosom. Carefully he lifted Jessie from Roni's arms, then laid the sleeping child down in the middle of his king-size bed and propped pillows on either side of her. He knew that Roni had risen and was watching him closely.

"I should get busy assembling her baby bed." The pieces of the white Jenny Lind bed he'd brought back from Alicia's apartment in Abilene still lay stacked in a heap in the front parlor among the other debris of Jessie's arrival.

"She might sleep better," Roni agreed cautiously.

He knew they weren't really talking about baby beds. "Come on. I need a beer."

With Roni trailing after him, he stalked into the kitchen, pulled open the refrigerator door and reached for a dark brown bottle. "Want one?"

She shook her head, moving about his kitchen with easy familiarity, automatically putting away the forgotten sacks of groceries. She set the kettle on the stove and opened a box of herbal tea.

"I'd rather have this." Though she tried to keep her voice light, he could hear the strain in it. "And it's rather unflattering, you know, for you to be so flabbergasted. Hadn't you ever thought that you and I—that we..."

"No," he said flatly, twisting open the beer bottle. "I hadn't."

She threw a tea bag into a mug and turned to him with a belligerent tilt to her chin. "Well, how... how very *unchivalrous* of you. All the same, it makes perfect sense, if you'll just think."

"Sense?" He snorted. "Curly, you've gone loco."

Her cheeks brightened again, but she went on doggedly. "It's the solution you need for Jessie, Sam. We both adore her. Together we can make the kind of home she deserves, and frankly, there are worse ways to start off married life than by being good friends."

"I don't know what to say." He shook his head, dazed. "You'd do that for Jessie?"

"I'd do it for *me*. I'm sick of living alone."

Sam heard the plaintiveness in her tone and realized he'd been too caught up in his own concerns to see that his ever-upbeat pal was struggling with her own brand of loneliness. Straddling a kitchen chair, he took a drink of his beer and stared down at the bottle. "I'll admit it's no picnic for me, either."

"I've always wanted a home and a family, and I know you have, too. But things just haven't worked out as either of us planned." Sighing, she leaned her trim hips against the kitchen counter and warmed her hands around her mug as though fighting off a chill. She was silent a long moment, gazing down into the steaming liquid. "I suppose in a way I'll always love Jackson, but he couldn't give me what I truly wanted and needed."

"I know that."

"But you can, Sam." She lifted her eyes, and her words were earnest. "If Jessie is your second chance at that kind of life, she's my first and last chance. I want her, more than anything I've ever wanted. I know we could be the kind of parents she needs and bring her up right with love and security."

"You wouldn't be getting much out of the deal."

"That's where you're wrong. We'd be a family. That's more than enough." Catching his skeptical glance, she set her mug aside and persisted. "Neither of us is getting any younger, Sam. Just think of it as a practical solution to the problem. We both work at home, with flexible schedules, so Jessie's needs could come first, without having to depend on housekeepers and day care. And you've been too damn proud to accept my offer to use my daddy's pasture-land. Married, we can combine our assets and build something permanent together for Jessie on the Lazy Diamond. It's perfect. We'd all benefit.''

"I think you're forgetting something." Deliberately, he drained his beer, set the bottle down on the table, then rose and came to stand in front of her. "What about sex?"

She swallowed. "What about it?"

"Don't play dumb, Curly." He cupped her shoulders and let his thumbs trace the delicate line of her collarbone. "You know what I mean."

"Can't we cross that bridge when we come to it?"

Catching her around the waist, he jerked her up against him, bending to nuzzle the flower-fragrant crook of her neck. His unexpected touch evoked a shiver and a gasp from her, and he bared his teeth in a wolfish grin, muttering, "I think we just did."

Her fingers grasped his forearms for balance. "You're not going to scare me off, if that's what you're trying to do."

He drew back, giving her a hard look, then pressed himself suggestively against her middle in blatant mimicry of the act they were discussing. "A man wants a willing woman in his bed, Veronica Jean, not a martyr."

Her breathing accelerated, and she hesitated, licking her lips. "I—I'm not unwilling."

That set him aback. Sam admitted to himself that he'd crowded her to show her just how asinine this idea of hers was, that he was no sexless eunuch to be dismissed out of hand, but her response was forcing him to see her in a new light. Damn, he knew she was a beautiful, desirable woman, but he'd never allowed himself to think of her like that. Those had been the unspoken rules. She was just Curly, who'd always been there for him. Anything else felt strange and unnatural, didn't it?

Releasing her, he stepped back a pace, rubbing his hand over his nape in consternation. "We've never had those feelings toward each other, Curly."

"Perhaps not. But we've got a lot more going for us than most couples—trust, dependability, a wealth of knowledge and history together. The other could evolve naturally, if we wanted it to."

"And if it doesn't?" he challenged.

"Companionship and mutual respect are important, too." She shrugged uncomfortably. "And we're both adults with no illusions about love left to shatter. As long as we're both discreet, outside, er—friendships shouldn't be a problem, if it came to that."

He laughed harshly. "How very modern of you."

She flushed again. "Look, making a stable family environment for Jessie is the prime consideration here, isn't it? What's to keep us from going on just as we've been doing the last few days?"

"You think keeping things platonic would work?"

"It has so far," she pointed out with irrefutable logic. Then she smiled, a little tender, a little bemused, cajoling him into temptation. "Come on, Sam. Let's do it for Jessie. We're comfortable together, like a favorite pair of old boots. It wouldn't be that hard. In some ways, we're already like an old married couple."

"You mean passion on the back burner, constant bickering and taking each other for granted?"

She chuckled. "Something like that."

Sam's lips twitched in an answering grin. *She never fails to make me smile.*

For an instant he resisted acknowledging a decision that he'd already made deep down inside. The alternative—giving up the baby girl who'd stolen his heart, and losing Roni's respect—was unthinkable. And a part of him yearned for the connection and continuity of a family just as fiercely as Roni did.

Hell, she knew what she was getting into. Knew him for the lunkheaded cowpuncher and struggling rancher he was, knew small-town life and all that came with it. She'd taken her knocks, too, and wouldn't expect rainbows and miracles every minute, nor would she light out at the first hint of rough going.

It might look a bit crazy to the outside world, but it was a logical plan that solved their present situation without a lot of sentimental fuss, which suited Sam right down to his boots. They could forge an honorable life together, for Jessie and for themselves. All it took was a little courage.

"Well," he drawled, "that's not the greatest sales pitch I ever heard, but I suppose I can live with it."

Her eyes widened. "You mean it?"

"I can't believe I'm saying this, but yes, ma'am, thank you kindly. I accept your proposal." His words went a trifle ragged with an admission straight from his own heart. "Hell, Curly, I'm damned tired of being alone, too."

"Oh, Sam!" She threw herself against his broad chest. Sam closed his arms around her, enjoying the warmth of her closeness.

"And you'll tell the Newtons that Jessie is ours?" she asked, her voice tremulous.

"Yes. Ours." The very words made his throat tighten.

Roni relaxed against him and stood quietly in the circle of his arms, her cheek pressed over his heart. "We'll just take it day by day, okay?"

"Sure. After all, what we're doing is nobody's business but our own. Let the world draw its own conclusions."

"Agreed. You won't be sorry, I promise."

He gave a mock groan. "Oh, I'm sure I will be, trying to keep up with two women in my life. And I know you'll have your own share of regrets—"

"Oh, no."

"—but we'll make it together, God willing."

"Yes," she breathed, "God willing."

"Now are you scared?"

Roni toyed with the pearl snap on his shirt, and he felt her tremble. "Maybe just a little." Raising her head, she looked up into his face with a smile so brilliant, it took his breath. "But I'm more than content with what I'm getting out of this bargain. Know why?"

Dazzled, his answer was monosyllabic. "Uh—"

"Because I'm getting a husband who cooks, that's why. Now, Mr. Preston, about those steaks..."

"No, indeed, you are most certainly *not* getting married in the judge's chambers. That's barbaric!"

"But, Mother—"

"Put Sam on the line."

Helplessly, Roni held out the receiver of the kitchen phone. "She wants to talk to you."

"Uh-oh." Sam traded the wrench he'd used to assemble Jessie's baby bed for the phone, his blue eyes sparkling. The dishes from their steak supper lay soaking in the sink, and Jessie still slept, unaware that she was in the process of acquiring parents. "I guess I'm in big trouble, huh?"

"Be serious, Sam," Roni pleaded. "She's talking about a real wedding."

Cupping a hand over the receiver, he cocked one sandy eyebrow. "Well, that's what it's going to be, isn't it?"

Exasperated, she blew a dark curl off her forehead. "You know what I mean—a church, ushers, a cake with a *foun-*

*tain,* for gosh sakes. Tell her we insist on a quiet ceremony. This Saturday. In Judge Holt's chambers as we planned.''

Nodding, Sam raised the receiver to his mouth. ''Hello, Miss Carolyn. Yes, well, thank you, I think so. I—yes, ma'am.''

Roni chewed her lip anxiously, but a dozen or more ''Yes, ma'am's'' was the limit to Sam's conversation with her mother. Before she knew it, he hung up, turning to her with an apologetic shrug. ''She's so excited about our news that she and Jinks are driving in tonight. To get things organized. She says she's bringing you her wedding dress.''

Roni buried her face in her hands with a groan. ''I knew we should have eloped.''

''Miss Carolyn knew I wouldn't deprive her of the pleasure of seeing her only child properly married off.'' Sam came up behind Roni and began to massage her tense shoulders. ''What could I say?''

''*Nein.* Uh-uh. No way, José.'' She gave a sigh of pleasure as Sam's deft fingers unkinked the knots in her neck, then suddenly straightened with a gasp of realization. ''Oh, God! I'll have to go home. Mother wouldn't understand the situation here. That is—''

''Relax, Curly.'' Sam gently drew her back against himself, still working on her shoulders. His voice was low in her ear, and his warm breath tickled her skin. ''I'm not going to do anything that will embarrass you, including giving your mother reason to believe we've been sleeping together without benefit of clergy.''

Roni gulped, and her face flamed. ''Uh, at our ages, she's liable to draw her own conclusions anyway.''

''Exactly. On the other hand, we can hardly declare we're both pure as the driven snow in that department without provoking a lot of nosy questions. The circumstances of our marriage are nobody's business but our own, but propriety demands certain conventions. I've got no objections to keeping up appearances and going through the rituals." Turning her to face him, he lifted her chin with his thumb and met her gaze. "It's the least I can do for the woman who's to be my wife."

Roni caught her breath. The rugged face above her was as dear and familiar to her as her own, but until this moment she had never truly appreciated the depth of the decency and respect with which Sam lived his life. The contrast between his and Jackson Dial's philosophy could not have been greater. And now she was to be an integral part of Sam's life, the recipient of his caring concern and commitment. It was a prospect that boded well for her future contentment and produced a betraying surge of emotion.

"Now you just stop that, Sam Preston," she murmured. "You're going to make me cry."

"Lord, don't do that again." His expression was faintly alarmed. "I couldn't handle that twice in one day."

She chuckled softly. "You've got a lot to learn about women, then. And if my mother gets too bossy about this wedding, you're liable to get worse than a few tears from me."

He tugged a lock of her hair. "Aw, Curly, it'll be all right."

"Easy for you to say," she muttered darkly.

"Look, you're going to be too busy to brood. I was thinking if I cleaned out the storeroom you could use it as your studio."

"It does have that huge window," she said thoughtfully. "I'd like that, if you don't mind."

"Mind? We're going to be partners now, Curly. You'll have as much right to this house as I do. And that's not all. We've got to get the license and rings, make the wedding arrangements, and move the rest of your things over here, not forgetting that you've still got a deadline and I've got a thousand head of cattle to move to spring pastures."

"Oh, golly." She swallowed. "Rather a daunting lot, isn't it?"

"I'll say. So you go home and keep your mother and Jinks company until Saturday. Jessie and I'll manage."

Roni frowned and shook her head. "No, she's just getting accustomed to both of us. I'll see her tucked in at bedtime and be back for breakfast. If I disappeared completely now, just like Alicia did, it might upset her all over again."

Sam nodded. "I see your point. We'll just do a bit of juggling. No big deal."

"And Mother is dying to meet her. I'm sure once she sets eyes on our little hellion, I won't be able to separate them." Roni smiled wryly. "This is quite a bit to absorb for my mother, you know—her old-maid daughter married, a new son-in-law and a grandbaby. She's rather boggled, but that won't keep her from trying to run the show."

"Nothing we can't handle, Curly, my girl." Laughing, Sam gave her a friendly squeeze of encouragement. "Nothing we can't handle."

Sam didn't know exactly when things got out of hand. But they had. Definitely.

On the finest Saturday afternoon April had ever produced in Flat Fork, Texas, he found himself in his Sunday best suit, his favorite boots polished to a high gloss, waiting to marry his best friend.

And not in the relative privacy of Judge Holt's office, either. No, sirree, Roni's mother had taken one look around and promptly moved the service to the rose garden behind the Methodist church. Between the bower of fresh green ferns and the natural profusion of early scarlet and pink blossoms, Sam had to admit the setting was very pretty. But whose idea had it been for Angel Morales's cousin to play "The Wedding March" on his twelve-string guitar? And where had all these people come from?

Sam swallowed hard and tried to appear calm before the crowd of expectant faces seated on rows of folding chairs, standing on the grass behind them and spilling onto the sidewalks beyond. What was to have been a quiet ceremony with a handful of guests had mushroomed as word spread. While it was gratifying that his and Roni's friends and neighbors would want to share in the happy occasion, Sam was more than a bit taken aback by this outpouring of goodwill. Or curiosity. He caught Reverend Burdett's eye and received a nod of encouragement just as Angel's cousin launched into a flamenco crescendo.

A chorus of "oohs" made him look up. Coming down the narrow paved path between the rows of chairs were Roni's two attendants, Krystal in a pale pink, midcalf sundress, pushing a stroller in which sat his little redhead, looking adorable in her own pink smock. Both wore dainty wreaths of fresh spring flowers and baby's breath in their hair, but Jessie's was already tilted at a rakish angle over one eye and she was doing her best to detach and demolish what she could reach of it.

Laughter rippled over the crowd, and Sam grinned, proud as any father at his newly acquired daughter's obvious charm and beauty. Jessie spotted him just as Krystal parked the stroller in place before the minister.

"Da!" she announced in delight, then offered Sam the aster crushed in her pudgy fist.

Carolyn beamed, and the other guests murmured approval as Sam bent and gravely accepted the gift. Then he caught sight of the vision at the other end of the path and totally forgot who he was, what he was doing and how to breathe.

*My God, she's gorgeous.*

Clutching her stepfather's arm, Roni came to him to the sultry beat of a Spanish guitar, her brown eyes wide, her rosy lips parted in a shy smile. She'd let her hair fly wild and loose for once, and the whiskey-dark locks curled and undulated in a vibrant halo around her face to her shoulders. Another simple flowery wreath crowned her head and ivory ribbons floated down her back.

Belatedly, Sam realized how rarely he'd seen her in a dress, much less such a purely feminine creation. The lines of the ivory lace gown decreed an earlier fashion age, but it could have been created especially to showcase Roni's beauty, from its scalloped neckline to the fitted bodice that lovingly cupped her full breasts to the graceful drape of the calf-length skirt that revealed the seductive flare of her hips. She was regal and romantic, a fairy queen out of a man's most dangerous dream, a mischievous and beguiling Titania.

And he didn't know her at all. Fear bolted through him. *What am I doing?*

Jinks Robinson, graying and affable, briefly bussed Roni's cheek, then handed her over to Sam and went to sit with his wife. Bemused, Sam wordlessly offered Roni the crushed aster that Jessie had given him. She hesitated only momentarily, taking it and tucking it into the bouquet of white roses he'd given her while a collective sigh rose from the wedding guests.

*Who is this man?* Roni fumbled in the bouquet with trembling fingers, utterly shocked by the tall, solemn stranger at her side. Was this her Sam, this man with shoulders broad enough to block out the sun? Rays of golden light trickled through the treetops and gleamed on his fair hair, brushed ruthlessly into an unfamiliar and alarming orderliness. He was archangel and conqueror, warrior and master, and masculinity radiated from him in powerful waves, tempting and frightening and foreign.

Panic clawed at Roni's throat. *Oh, God, what am I doing here?*

A burble of baby giggles broke the spell. Chortling, cheerfully shredding her headdress, Jessie babbled up at Sam and Roni, demanding conversation. As one, they bent and murmured to her. Then they caught each other's eye. Recognition was instantaneous, and all constraint melted, for the purpose behind their union was clear again—a tiny redheaded girl who needed them both. Relieved, Sam took Roni's hand firmly in his own and received an answering squeeze that made the corner of his mouth tilt upward.

"Ready, Curly?" he murmured.

Smiling, she nodded, and they took their places before the minister.

"Dearly beloved . . ."

*I, Veronica Jean, take you, Samuel . . .*

*. . . to have and to hold . . .*

*. . . for better, for worse . . .*

*. . . with this ring, I thee wed . . .*

And then it was almost over, the unfamiliar weight of gold bands binding their lives together, and they bowed their heads as the guitarist's voice lifted in the liquid melody of a beloved prayer.

"What are all these people doing here?" Roni asked in a whisper.

Sam's reply was equally low. "Came for the best show in Flat Fork today, I guess."

"But there's so *many*."

"Yeah." He grinned and gave her a wink. "Hope there's enough cake."

That provoked a flurry of giggles that Roni had a hard time constraining. Luckily, the soloist had finished his last "Amen." Reverend Burdett's smiled was indulgent, for he'd seen many euphoric couples in his time, and this next part was his personal favorite of all his duties.

"Now, Sam, you may kiss your bride."

Two pairs of sparkling eyes met. Two hearts flipped over. Two reasonably competent adults mentally kicked themselves for not remembering, for not even *once* practicing this most important symbol. And a sea of curious, expectant onlookers was watching to see what would happen next.

Gamely, Sam took Roni's shoulders, bending his head for a quick and courteous peck, but then a devilish gleam sparked his blue eyes.

"Aw, hell, Curly," he growled. "Let's give 'em their money's worth."

Sliding one arm around her waist, he gathered her close and buried his other hand in the curls at her nape. Holding her still, he slanted his head and covered her mouth, catching her startled gasp with his lips, inhaling the sweetness of her breath in an intoxicating rush. And then his intention changed, for her lips quivered and parted, and forgetfulness overcame him as pure sensation plunged him into oblivion.

*I didn't know... sweet, so hot and sweet... Curly!*

Her hands came up to loop about his neck, pulling him closer, and the bouquet she held enveloped them in a cloud of perfume. A deep trembling struck her soul with wonder. *Sam, what are you doing to me?* Whatever it was, she couldn't get enough, and she strained against him, opening for him without conscious choice, following an instinct as old as the ages.

Boldly he tasted her, wild honey and thyme, spice and sweetness, more addictive and exciting than anything he'd ever known. When the tip of her tongue met his, both aggressive exploration and tender enticement, he groaned and she shivered.

"Amen."

The minister's good-natured reminder of the proper place for such things broke them apart, blushing and red-faced amid the teasing laughter of the onlookers. The guitarist began a celebratory song, and the guests rose and congratulated the happy couple in an impromptu receiving line.

"Darling!" Carolyn enveloped her daughter in a warm hug. "Every blessing. You've made me so happy. I always knew the two of you were just meant for each other."

Still dazed by the onslaught of unexpected sensations Sam's passionate kiss had stirred, Roni accepted her mother's hugs and salutations with a glazed look and blazing cheeks. Meant for each other? Is that what people thought? But somehow, something elemental had changed in the blink of an eye and the touching of lips, and now Roni didn't know even what she thought herself. Her heart still pounded, and a heady taste, the essence of Sam himself, lingered on her lips, branding her, unnerving her, making her wish that they hadn't been interrupted.

Which was shameful, for hadn't they agreed this wasn't something they needed or wanted right now? Dear God, how had things gotten so out of control so quickly? she groaned inwardly. He'd meant it as a joke, hadn't he?

Jinks hugged Roni, then passed her on to Krystal, who was holding Jessie. "I knew you were holding out on me." Krystal laughed her teasing accusation. "Immune to Sam's charms, my eye. You lucky dog."

"Krystal, please!" Roni's cheeks were scarlet. To hide her embarrassment, she took Jessie and hastily tried to straighten what was left of her headdress.

Her friend gave her a sassy wink. "Enjoy, I say."

Meanwhile, Jinks had moved on to shake Sam's hand, his booming voice carrying clearly. "Congratulations, my boy! That's quite a gal you've caught yourself. You be darned good to her, you hear?"

Roni barely stifled a groan. Was all this gushing by her relatives necessary?

"Yes, sir. That's a promise," Sam was saying. He caught her eye then, and though his words were for Jinks, the amusement in his look was shared with Roni. Somewhat reassured, Roni turned away to greet another well-wisher.

With an effort, Sam tore his gaze from his bride and tried to douse the flame that had stirred within him by putting on his affable cowboy grin, the one that had hidden his true feelings from rambunctious steers and drunken bullies and demanding females for so long and so well. He hoped it worked equally well on curious wedding guests, for he sure as hell had no explanations—for himself or for anyone else—for the conflagration that had nearly gotten out of hand between him and Roni at the altar.

Holy Jehoshaphat! What a danged fool he was. His lusty reactions were likely to scare off the girl before they even got a good start on this thing.

Shaking the hands of innumerable well-wishers, Sam's gaze kept going back to the woman laughing and accepting congratulations nearby. They milled through the crowd, visiting and showing off Jessie, conscious in a way like never before of each other's every movement. Whenever she caught his eye, her color rose and her gaze slid swiftly away again. Sam inwardly cursed the streak of cussedness that had made him pull such a damn-fool stunt.

But it was odd that, until the moment he'd kissed her, he'd never really noticed her mouth, the soft shape of it, the lush lower lip that hinted of latent sensuality. Now he couldn't stop looking at it, nor thinking about the way she tasted. The way she chewed at the corner of it when she was worried drove him crazy. And her smile... There couldn't be a more perfect mouth with a more perfect smile in all the universe. Just made for a man to explore...

Sam reined his galloping thoughts to a reluctant halt. *Preston, you're crazy. Cut it out.*

*I must be going crazy,* Roni thought. Though she carried on perfectly sensible conversations, she had no notion of what she said. But when Sam spared her the merest look, she knew it instantly and felt a flush all the way to her core. And when his gaze fell to her mouth, her lips tingled in remembered ecstasy and longing.

This sensitivity was as unexpected as it was unwelcome, she told herself sternly. What if this sudden awareness was all on her part? How humiliating. Sam hadn't bargained for that. No, she'd simply have to get control of these surging emotions. They were no doubt due to the strains of the day, not anything more than a passing physical awareness that would soon die back down where it belonged when things returned to normal. After all, they'd agreed. And Sam was a man of his word.

*You're a man who stands by his word, Preston. Forget it. Forget how good Roni tasted, or you're liable to drive her away.* Sam's mouth went dry with fear at the thought, and inexplicably stayed that way, even through the toasting with the champagne Jinks had brought, through the cake tasting and the bouquet throwing.

Because sooner or later, he knew he was going to be alone with Roni—with his new wife—and for the life of him, agreement or not, he didn't know how he was going to resist the temptation to kiss her again.

"Maybe someday he'd be able to trust her again. To go along with that, his new life would ... For the first time in months, he almost felt carefree as he turned and their glances locked..."

# Four

"**Y**ou sure you don't mind about the honeymoon?"

"No, Sam."

"Maybe we should have driven into Fort Worth for the night. It's still not too late. We could—"

"Sam?"

"Huh?"

"Put a cork in it." Roni stepped out of her wedding pumps and pressed her aching arches to the cool kitchen floor with a soft sigh of relief. Outside, the crickets sang their night song in the sweet spring grass. "We agreed it was better to come home. She's absolutely worn-out."

"Yeah." Sam cuddled a drooping Jessie against his shoulder, ignoring the damp circle her drool made on his shirt. He'd discarded his jacket and tie long before, and his sun-streaked hair had returned to its usual finger-ruffled disorder. Lifting a hand, he rubbed his thumb over Roni's cheekbone. "She's not the only one who looks tuckered out."

Roni froze under his unexpected caress, and her stomach flipped over. She forced a breathy laugh. "It's not nice to call your wife a hag."

Sam's eyes darkened to the deep blue of a mountain lake. "You're beautiful. Surely you know that?"

Rattled beyond belief, Roni moved away from his touch, trying to find her equilibrium with another laugh. "And you've had too much champagne, cowboy. As weddings go, ours was really something, don't you think?"

"Yeah, something."

The husky timbre of his voice and the heat in his eyes evoked a wayward memory of their bridal kiss—*the kiss,* she labeled it in her mind now—as well as a stab of panic that made her chatter nervously.

"The cake actually tasted good, but I was glad I overruled Mother about the fountain. And wasn't the music unique? But Jessie stole the show, of course."

Sam grinned slightly. "Of course."

"And wasn't it nice to have everyone just turn up like that?" The hem of Roni's lace dress swished about her calves as she unpinned her headpiece, then set it on the table next to her wedding bouquet. Her fingers lingered on the ivory ribbons. "Something to press into a memory book."

"I certainly won't forget the send-off. Thanks to Krystal's enthusiasm, I think I've still got rice in my drawers."

She smirked at him. "Ouch. That smarts."

"A small price to pay for those wedding gifts in the back of the pickup." His expression held a teasing twinkle. "Not a bad haul, actually."

"Just like a man to be so materialistic." Absently, she curled the tail of a ribbon around and around her index finger. "It makes me feel something of a fraud."

"Aw, now, Curly..."

She looked up at him, her dark eyes wide and fathomless. "We've begun under rather false pretenses, haven't we, Sam?"

"There's nothing false about making a home together for Jessie," he said, his voice firm. "Don't you ever forget that. You're just feeling a little whacked-out, that's all."

"Perhaps you're right." She reached for the drowsy child. "Here, let me get her to bed."

"No, I'll see to her. You get comfortable. Take a hot bath or something."

Sam carried the baby off to her room, and Roni swallowed hard.

*Or something?*

What did Sam expect of her tonight? More importantly, what did she expect of herself? She honestly had no idea. It was their wedding night, after all. *As if I thought I could forget!* she groaned inwardly.

Swiftly she placed her bouquet and headdress in their protective bags and tucked them into the refrigerator for safekeeping. Later, she would hang them in the attic to dry, to have as an everlasting arrangement, maybe to fix them in a romantic Victorian bell jar. Her plans ground to a halt. The way the air seemed to sizzle whenever Sam came close, and the way her heart turned over at his touch were indications that she wasn't thinking straight at all.

Desperately, she tried to remember her arguments of just a few short days before, how things could develop slowly and naturally, how they were as comfortable as a pair of well-broken-in boots. Was she so naive? How could a few words spoken in front of a preacher have changed that?

And yet it appeared that they had, and she felt as though she were on a roller coaster gaining speed down the first tall hill, faster and faster to a destiny that was as unknown as it was thrilling.

And terrifying.

Heart pounding against her chest wall, Roni knew it was time to put on the brakes. *Now.* Out of sight, out of mind. Time to cool off before they made a dreadful mistake they'd only regret in the morning after emotions settled and the champagne fumes dissipated. The plan flickered to life in her brain—a bath, a plea of fatigue, tucking herself into her solitary twin bed in the safety of her new daughter's nursery. A cowardly path, perhaps, but eminently prudent, at least at the moment.

With the sound of Sam's deep voice drifting down the hall from Jessie's room, Roni hurried to the parlor where her overnight bag sat, rummaged in it for a concealing sleep shirt and her toiletries bag, then hurried toward the bathroom. She locked the door behind her with a sigh of relief, then chided herself for acting like a trembling virgin. She was a mature woman, she reminded herself sternly, able to make competent decisions, and what she wanted right now was a long, hot bath. In fact, she planned to stay in it until her skin resembled a prune, and Sam Preston was sound asleep.

The tub was a relic, scarred and stained with rust. Roni twisted the knobs, cursing and tugging at the stubborn hot water spigot until it gave and a stream of rusty water poured into the bath. The whole house needed replumbing, but at the moment, all she could do was pour in her foaming bath oil and hope for the best. Roni pulled off the blue garter Krystal had given her for luck, then stripped out of her panty hose and half-slip. She reached to unfasten her dress, and her eyes widened with dismay.

"Oh, hell!"

Straining, she could only reach the top three covered buttons of a line that ran down her spine from her nape to her hips. Her mother had helped her dress, and it had never occurred to Roni that without assistance she was trapped in her own wedding gown. And the only assistance available to her now was Sam himself.

There had to be a way. Grimacing, Roni craned her arms backward until she thought they'd pop from their sockets, but only succeeded in freeing one more button.

The bubbles in the bathtub were almost overflowing. With a sound of frustration, Roni twisted the taps off, struggling momentarily again with the hot water spigot before forcing it shut. She caught sight of a back brush hanging on a nail and tried to pry another button loose with its long handle. She nearly had it free when she heard the awful ripping sound of a seam giving way.

Panting, Roni dropped the brush and tried to assess the damage. This had been her mother's wedding dress, and now hers, and in the back of Roni's mind she'd already been planning for Jessie to wear it someday, too. There was no way she was going to ruin it out of a misguided sense of modesty. Defeated, she realized she would have to ask Sam for help.

Blowing a damp curl out of her face, Roni spoke to herself in the steamy mirror. "All right. Be casual. Nothing unusual here. Just a friend helping a friend."

Taking a deep breath, she unlocked the door, then hesitated in the hall. Sam tiptoed out of Jessie's room a moment later, carefully pulling the door shut behind him in the way of all parents who prayed that their offspring would continue to sleep. It might have been a comical position on a man with less stature, but on Sam the attitude was watchful, protective and somehow very attractive. Roni felt her mouth go dry.

Hand on the doorknob, he looked up at her in surprise. "I thought you were in the tub."

"I'm trying, but that spigot was being stubborn again. It's really kind of dangerous, so could you fix it soon?"

"Yeah, I've been meaning to get to that."

"And I'm having a little trouble..." She shrugged sheepishly and pointed at her back. "I can't—that is, uh, would you?"

"Sure." Hands on her shoulders, he turned her, then went to work on the buttons. "I swear, female garb can sure be mystifying. Who'd think a garment you can't get into or out of by yourself is a good idea?"

*A woman who wants her husband to touch her.* The thought caught Roni by surprise and heated her skin. Or perhaps it was the brush of Sam's callused fingers that splayed electricity along her nerve endings. Was it her imagination, or had his progress slowed, so that he seemed to linger on the last few buttons gracing the curve of her spine? And did he realize that except for her lacy demibra, she was naked beneath the dress?

Roni's breathing accelerated, but when she went to move away Sam forestalled her by sliding a hand through the opening of the gown to rest in the indention of her waist. Startled, Roni looked over her shoulder, only to be snagged by the intensity of Sam's blue gaze. The pressure of his fingers on her bare skin increased, spreading down over the jut of her hipbone. Over her token resistance he pulled her back flush against himself.

"You're as skittish as a newborn filly, Miss Curly."

"Sam..." Her breath clogged in her throat as his gaze fell to her mouth, and her knees went weak. "You know this isn't a good idea."

"Why?"

"You're just curious."

"Uh-huh." His other hand skimmed over her shoulder, easing under her scalloped neckline to explore the tender skin stretched over her collarbone. "Aren't you?"

"No."

"Liar. You're wondering just like I am."

"Wondering what?"

"If that kiss was really as good as we both thought it was."

"You're imagining things." She licked her lips. "I—my bathwater's getting cold."

Light flared behind his eyes and his voice was thick. "The hell with it."

Catching her chin between his fingers, he tipped her face up and settled his mouth over hers. His lips were warm and sweet and wild, and Roni melted. But even that surrender wasn't enough for Sam. He turned her to face him, his hands pushing her shoulders against the wall, his mouth never leaving hers. He insinuated a knee between her legs, pressing her skirts in a most intimate and erotic glide of satin and lace.

Roni moaned, feeling the urgency building in him, helpless to stop it, not certain that she even wanted to. Grasping her sagging gown to her breasts, she could do nothing but hold on as sensation washed over her in waves. Overwhelmed, she parted her lips at his demand, gasping as his tongue found hers and performed nimble and intoxicating tricks, sweeping the cavern of her mouth, striking her dumb and blind at the burgeoning power of her own need.

He raised his head, peppering tiny kisses at the corner of her mouth, the curve of her jawbone. Her chest heaved with the effort to find enough oxygen to survive. "Sam, I can't...breathe."

"Good." His voice was muffled as he nibbled at the tender curve of her neck, riffling goose bumps down every extremity. "Neither can I."

"It's too soon," she gasped in growing panic. "Oh, stop! I can't think."

"Then don't."

His low chuckle was almost a growl, pleased and infinitely male and utterly alarming, for Roni knew instinctively it was the sound of a man claiming his mate. When he bent to possess her lips again, she latched desperately on to a handful of the hair curling at his nape and tugged hard to gain his attention.

"Sam! You're scaring me."

He poised a mere hairbreath from her lips, his gaze dark and murky with passion. In the blink of an eye, the clouds retreated, and he looked at her, clear-eyed, with something akin to horror in his expression.

"My God, Curly, I'm sorry!"

He let her go so quickly, she almost sagged to the floor, and would have if his hands hadn't come up to steady her elbows. For an endless moment, they stared into each other's eyes, shocked and shaken by the volatility of the brief encounter.

There was nothing to say. Nothing that *could* be said. The sound of a small girl's sleepy fretting finally penetrated their bubble of bewilderment.

"You—you'd better go to her," Roni said huskily.

"Yes." Slowly, as if his hands were having trouble obeying his brain's commands, Sam released her and took a step back.

"I—I'll finish my bath."

"Uh, sure." He rubbed the back of his neck, consternation and embarrassment making his features stiff. "What we both, uh, need is a good night's rest."

"Right." She backed toward the bathroom, holding the dress to keep it from falling off her shoulders. The lace felt scratchy to her sensitized palms, her breasts full and itchy. "See you in the morning, then."

"Yeah. Good night."

Roni turned the lock on the bathroom door, not knowing whether to laugh or cry. She let her wedding dress drop, unhooked her bra, then stepped into the bathtub. The bubbles had melted into nothing but an oil slick on the surface and the water was cool, but she scarcely noticed, for her bemused brain was too busy working on a new and most startling revelation.

If truth be told, she *had* been wondering about a repeat of her wedding kiss, just as Sam said. Well, it had happened, and now she didn't have to wonder any longer. The second kiss wasn't as good as the first. No, to the detriment of any peace of mind she ever hoped to possess, she had to admit the truth.

It was even better.

Sam Preston was in big trouble, and he knew it.

A week into his second marriage, after a blistering Texas afternoon of alternately cursing and praying over the Lazy Diamond's ailing cattle truck, he was hot, tired and dirty. Not to mention raw and bloody across the knuckles from banging into the engine block. Maybe the damn thing would run a little longer. Maybe.

Sam stomped up the porch steps of the ranch house, mentally calculating the possibilities. If the truck died for good, it would practically put him out of the rodeo stock business, for there was no extra cash to replace the vehicle, and his line of credit down at the local bank was just about nil. In fact, five years after his divorce, he was only beginning to dig the ranch out of the financial morass left over from Shelly's settlement, and every setback—from a worn-out vehicle to a bull he couldn't replace—was critical.

Reaching for the handle of the screen door, Sam came up short as a flutter of bright-colored fabric caught his eye. Mouthing a curse of pure frustration, he glared at the short line strung between two porch posts and the delicate feminine laundry clothes-pinned to it—silky teddies and little scraps of lacy panties and a heart-stopping array of mysterious female undergarments guaranteed to drive a man slap out of his mind. Which is where he was going—fast.

Good God, who would have ever guessed that Curly hid all that fancy, female livery under her jeans every day? Shaking his head, Sam went inside. Every other problem in his life paled when compared to the fact that he had the hots for his own wife—and there was nothing he could do about it.

For the moment.

Setting his hat on a peg, he used the bootjack to shuck out of his boots, ripped open the snaps on his grease-stained work shirt and tugged it free of his waistband. From somewhere in the house, he could hear water running, and there was an aroma coming from the oven that made his empty belly rumble.

There were other evidences of feminine occupation creeping into his house, too. Ruffled pot holders with cows' faces on them by the stove. A teal rug at the back door. Some kind of strange-looking modern statue on the coffee table in the parlor, and a pile of art books nestled up beside his stacks of *Western Horseman* and *Hoof and Horn*.

They were finding a routine with Jessie, too, from bathing to naptime to a bout of real restlessness just the night before that had kept Roni hovering to the wee hours. Despite those demands, Roni had already managed to rough out her cover illustration in her new studio. Yeah, his and

Roni's everyday lives were meshing okay. If only they could get this relationship thing figured out as easily.

What had seemed so sensible when first discussed had turned out to be a Pandora's box as far as Sam was concerned. He couldn't quite explain, even to himself, how a couple of kisses—surprising as they were—had changed the way he looked at Roni. All he knew was that she was his now, legally and morally, and—dammit—all he could think about was taking her to bed!

Too bad Roni wasn't of the same mind. Every time he'd come near her over the past seven days, she'd shied away from him like a skittish mare scenting a stallion. She wasn't hard to read—she just wasn't ready for that step. Maybe she wouldn't ever be. The thought made Sam groan. Was it too much for a husband to expect conjugal rights? Or was he just an oversexed SOB with gonads for brains and no self-control?

Grinding his teeth in frustration, Sam opened the refrigerator for a beer, letting the cool air waft over his sweaty chest. At least she'd gotten her wedding flowers out of the food crisper. And as hard as it was for him to reconcile how quickly his thinking about Roni had changed, no doubt she was having the same kind of difficulty. Any more displays of passion on his part were likely to scare her off permanently, and that was the last thing he wanted.

The trick was patience, a little wooing, some time for her to get used to the idea. She wasn't indifferent to him, that much was clear, so he could take some solace in that. And although patience had never been his strong suit, he was man enough to control his impulses until she was ready, considering what his reward could be—a hot physical relationship with a woman he admired and trusted. Not a bad return for the investment, he figured.

Taking a slug from his beer, he grimaced at the faintly bitter taste. Yeah, he could back off, keep his distance until Curly gave him some indication she was ready to pursue what had begun with a wedding kiss. And damned if he wouldn't do it, or die trying. It was just going to be hard waiting for it to happen, that was all. But since he had been in that physical state most of the past week, what else was new?

He headed for the parlor, thinking about flipping through some channels for some news and taking a load off his feet for a few minutes, then came up stock-still. "What the hell—?"

Someone had rearranged the furniture. *Someone* had shifted things around in a room that hadn't been changed in forty years. Plumped fat, flowery pillows and quilts on the old spring-weary sofa, tossed around baskets of silk flowers and greenery with an indiscriminate hand, and put a dad-gum Japanese paper fan in the fireplace, for gosh sakes! But worse than anything, someone had *taken his chair.*

His favorite chair. The old recliner he'd just in the past few years gotten perfectly broken in for his backside. Why, he and that chair had a *history,* a relationship, and it was gone! Vanished, banished, booted without so much as a by-your-leave, replaced by a dinky Queen Anne contraption that wouldn't hold up a flea, much less a hundred-eighty-pound rancher. Frustrations that had been simmering for a full week bubbled over like erupting lava.

"Curly!" He roared the name of the perpetrator of this final indignity in the voice of an enraged lion. "By God, woman, this time you've gone too far."

Sam stormed down the hall, pounded on the bathroom door and tried the knob. To his mild surprise, it flew open, startling Roni into an attitude of frozen incredulity as she leaned across the basin to smooth concealer under her tired eyes. She wore French-cut panties and a brief little scrap of nothing for a bra, both crusted with stretch lace and as red as Eve's apple. Neither left much to the imagination, cupping and molding her supple form like a lover's hand.

The sight of her tanned thighs pressed against the edge of the white porcelain sink, the scarlet lace, the innocent "O" of her surprised mouth, all struck a match to the smoldering bonfire of Sam's overstretched nervous system, flaring his temper out of control.

"Where the hell is it?" he shouted.

Bewilderment widened her eyes. "Where's what?"

"You know damn well what! By God, Curly, some things in a man's home are sacred—don't you know that?" Whipping a towel off the rack, he tossed it at her. "And put on some damn clothes. Are you trying to drive me crazy?"

Indignation sprouted bright color high on Roni's cheekbones as she caught the towel and draped it around herself. "I didn't ask you to come barging in here like a rodeo bull. And for your information, Mr. Preston, it isn't exactly a picnic for me to see you parading around at all hours of the day and night in just your skivvies."

"What—" Her counterattack made Sam splutter. "Hell, I live here."

Her chest heaved with righteous anger. "Well, so do I."

Frustratingly, there was no argument to that. "Just tell me what you did with my chair," he growled.

"Your—? You mean that old plaid relic taking up space in front of the hearth?"

"You know perfectly well which one."

Something devilish glinted in the depths of her brown eyes. "What if I told you Angel took it to the dump?"

"What?" Sam squawked, and his face went dark as thunder. "How long ago? Hell, now I'll have to go after it—"

Roni crossed her arms and gave him a bland look. "Only as far as the back porch."

Halfway to the door, Sam's head snapped around. "Huh?"

"Jessie wet the seat, so I pushed it out there to sun." Exasperation and anger sparked her voice with acid. "Don't you think I know what that stupid, ugly chair means to you, you lunkhead?"

"Uh." Robbed of his full head of steam, Sam rubbed his neck in consternation. "Jeez, Curly—"

"Now what have you done to yourself?" She grabbed his hand to inspect the bloody scrapes on his knuckles.

The gentleness of her touch contrasted with her sharp tone and left Sam feeling faintly unbalanced. "Uh, whacked it on the carburetor. It's nothing—"

"Shut up and get over here." Dropping the towel, she flung open the medicine cabinet and grabbed a brown bottle of hydrogen peroxide. Holding his hand over the basin, she doused the wound, ignoring his indrawn hiss at the sting. "I haven't got time for you to be such a baby."

Sam grimaced at the burning sensation on his skin. He was burning elsewhere, too, as his body responded to her semiclad and utterly delectable female form. He had a brief mental vision of himself bending her over the sink, slipping his fingers under the scarlet silk at her hips to explore an even silkier place. And her breasts, velvety globes nearly slipping from the sexy bra as she bent over his hand. All he'd have to do was reach out and... With a shudder, he searched for control, but Roni's next sentence jarred him out of the fantasy.

"I've got to get Jessie to Dr. Hazelton's before his office closes."

A chill of alarm raced up Sam's spine. "Jessie? Why? What—?"

Finishing her first aid, Roni wrapped his hand in a towel. "She's been cranky all day, and now she's running a fever."

"A fever! How much? What's wrong with her?"

"Hundred and one. And that's what I'm going to find out, just as soon as I can get on some clean clothes."

Roni's pointed look made Sam feel like a jackass who'd just had a temper tantrum. He dared one last glance at the seductive curve of her cleavage, then began to back out of the bathroom.

"Oh. Yeah, sure. Sorry. I'll go with you."

"Why? Don't you think I can handle it?"

"Well, I guess..."

"Guess?" She lost her temper. "Don't you think I can manage a simple trip to the doctor by myself? Are you telling me you don't trust me to be a good mother?"

Her instantaneous transformation to fury amazed him. "No, of course not. I mean, sure you are—"

"Well, then, get the hell out of my way and let me do my job." With that, she kicked the door shut in his face.

Sam stared at the wood and cursed himself for being every kind of fool. Yes, sir, all he had to have was a little patience, do a little wooing.

And he was off to a hell of a good start.

"Come on, sweetie," Roni begged. "Tell me what you want."

Jessie's whimper bounced off the walls of the examination cubicle, and she squirmed on Roni's lap, pushing aside the proffered pacifier. Her skin was burning up and her eyes looked glassy. She'd rejected a bottle, her blanket and her favorite rag doll in quick succession, and Roni was feeling frazzled and a little desperate.

"I know you don't feel well," she crooned, smoothing Jessie's thick russet curls. The baby arched against her grasp and whined softly, the sound breaking Roni's heart. There was a real talent to keeping a sick child distracted until the doctor showed up. Roni grabbed a tattered personality magazine from a basket beside her chair. "Look, let's read a story."

The rattle of paper and the colorful pictures caught Jessie's attention. Roni turned the pages, pointing out the doggies and the diamonds and the devilish smiles of the rich and famous. Roni turned another page of the magazine, and her mouth twisted sourly. "Oh, look, Jessie, here's a Hollywood snake."

Her finger tapped Jackson Dial's handsome features. A slinky blond starlet graced the filmmaker's arm as he made an appearance at some swank Los Angeles night spot. Roni pushed her hair out her face, feeling frumpy and tired and inadequate.

She turned the page with a resentful snap. There was another failure to live down. Despite all her love and loyalty, she'd never won a commitment from Jackson. Now she had made a commitment with Sam, but couldn't lure him to her bed. One hand tugging at her ear, the other tangled in a lock of Roni's hair, Jessie settled against her new mother, and they both gave tired sighs.

A sleepless night and disrupted day in which she hadn't accomplished one stroke of work on her cover illustration hadn't done much for Roni's frame of mind, but it was the strange and stilted confrontation with Sam that had really put her into a state of blue funk. For a thrilling moment when he'd first burst into the bathroom, she'd thought all the tiptoeing and circling that they'd done the past week was finally at an end—and then he'd started shouting about his stupid chair.

Roni groaned and mentally kicked herself yet again for panicking on her wedding night and refusing what Sam had so willingly offered. There she'd been, possessed of a man whom most women would agree was a stud, whose touch excited her incredibly, a man whom she knew would never hurt her, and one who'd made a public commitment to her—and she'd turned him down? On sober reflection, it was Roni's opinion that she'd been a fool. A monumental one, at that.

But it was a woman's prerogative to change her mind, right? Only from the way he kept his distance, it appeared Sam had exercised that right, too. Okay, so maybe he'd decided that consummating what was for all practical purposes a business relationship was a bad move. She couldn't fault him for listening to an argument she'd advocated.

But things had changed. You couldn't live intimately with someone without at least *thinking* about what it would be like to make love, could you? And the thought of making love with Sam left her breathless. Surely he felt the same tension? So why didn't he do something about it? For God's sake, she'd been standing in the bathroom practically naked, and he hadn't even made a pass at her! In fact, he'd even shuddered at her touch.

Did she repulse him to such an extent? Roni wondered miserably. What was the matter with her, anyway? Maybe she was simply missing some vital aspect as a woman, maybe she had some deficiency that kept her from attracting the right kind of man. Her spirits sank another notch.

She had to accept that she'd blown what might be the only chance she was going to get with Sam. Well, so be it, then. If she was finding their agreement harder to live with than she'd planned, then that was her cross to bear. What she was going through was obviously a period of adjustment. Sooner or later, the heat she felt would die back down to the warmth of pure friendship. In the meantime, she wouldn't embarrass Sam by panting after him like some moonstruck schoolgirl.

"Well, well. Who have we here?" Dr. Hazelton, sixty and stocky, bluff and balding, breezed into the examining room with a warm smile on his bespectacled face. "Hello, there, Veronica. What seems to be the trouble with little Jessie?"

"Doc." Roni dropped the magazine and rose to her feet. Jessie took one look at the stranger and burrowed her face into Roni's shoulder. "She's running a fever and won't eat. I don't know what's the matter. I've done everything—"

Dr. Hazelton reached for his stethoscope. "Relax, Mother. You haven't done anything wrong. Little girls get the sniffles all the time."

"But she's so miserable."

"Hmm. I shouldn't wonder." Dr. Hazelton pressed the stethoscope to Jessie's chest, then checked her nose and ears with quick, unruffled efficiency while keeping up a stream of conversation. "You don't look quite up to snuff yourself."

"I'm working under a tight deadline," she admitted, thinking about the unfinished cover. That she looked so haggard the doctor saw fit to comment on it, depressed Roni even more. What chance did she stand with Sam in this condition? She gave a wan smile. "It's taking me a while to get the hang of this mother thing, I guess."

"Sam not helping you at all?"

She answered truthfully. "No, that's not it. He's wonderful with Jessie. Of course, he's really busy during the day right now culling the herd and picking out the prime bulls.''

"Going after that rodeo contract, is he?" Ignoring Jessie's protests, he placed her on her back on the examining table and checked her throat with a tongue depressor. "So is Travis King, I hear. They ought to work together."

At the doctor's nod, Roni picked up the now-squalling baby to comfort, shaking her head. "Sam wouldn't hear of it. They don't get along."

"Still? After all this time?" The physician clucked at the antics of grown men. "Foolishness. It was an accident that killed Kenny, pure and simple. They were all pretty good friends, too. Seems a shame to hold on to a grudge like that just because Travis was driving that night."

Roni jiggled the sobbing baby. "Sometimes there's no talking to a man."

"Well, you talk to that one of yours, missy, and see that he gives you a hand," he ordered brusquely. "I see the first signs of maternal stress, and you're going to have your hands full for a few days."

Roni's eyes widened in alarm. "What's the matter with her?"

"Now don't get all panic-stricken. Just allergies and two of the worst infected ears I've seen this spring." He scribbled on a prescription pad and handed the paper to her. "But it's nothing antibiotics and some fever medicine won't help."

"Oh, thank goodness." The tension in her features relaxed a hair, but the hand she used to pat Jessie's back held a betraying tremble.

"You're doing a good job with her, Veronica," he said, already moving toward the door and his next patient.

That bit of praise revived Roni's flagging spirits a smidgeon. Yes, motherhood was certainly one area that she could excel in, especially considering that her heart overflowed with love whenever she gazed at Jessie. In fact, she'd make sure she was the best mother in all of Flat Fork. She knew how important this contract was to the Lazy Diamond, and she was going to see that Sam was able to concentrate on business instead of this latest domestic crisis. If he never looked on her as a desirable woman again, at least he'd admire her for a competent partner and helpmate.

"Trust your instincts, and call me if you have any questions or if she seems worse." Dr. Hazelton gave Roni an encouraging pat on the shoulder and a final word of warning. "Sometimes these things can be tricky."

Prescriptions clutched in her hand, resolve firmly in place, she nodded to the older man. "Thank you, Doc. Don't worry, I'll take care of everything."

# Five

---

*Tricky* wasn't the word for it.

Neither was *fatiguing, frustrating* or *ego-sapping*. No, after five days of nursing a one-year-old infant with two red ears, Roni knew that there truly weren't words in the English language to describe how she felt, except perhaps the old Texas saw, "drawn through a knothole backward."

Her hair was bundled in a frizzy ponytail, and she couldn't remember how long she'd been wearing, sleeping and trying to paint in the same oversize T-shirt and cutoff shorts. To make matters worse, Sam's cattle transport truck had broken down the night before and he'd been forced to spend the night stranded halfway between Flat Fork and Wichita. Although it was almost suppertime, he still hadn't made it home. Which was perhaps all to the good, since Roni was sure her haggard appearance was enough to scare off any man.

"Please, Jessie, honey, take your medicine."

Seated on the bed in the baby's nursery, Roni squinted her sandy eyes and poked a spoon loaded with pink syrup at the reluctant child. Jessie screwed up her rosebud mouth and swatted the spoon. Sticky pink spray splattered Roni, her shirt, the wall and the bed sheets.

"Jessie Marie Preston!" Surprise and frustration made Roni's voice harsher than she intended. She rose and plunked the child into her baby bed and raised the side with a violence that shook the whole contraption. "I've had quite enough of you, young lady!"

In stained gown and diaper, Jessie pulled to her tiny feet, clutched the plastic teething rail with her dimpled fists and let loose a howl of protest to raise the dead. Roni ignored her. She used the tail of her shirt to wipe the sticky droplets dripping down her chin, then stripped the splattered bedding down to the bare twin mattress.

Reaching for the medicine bottle again, she grimly refilled the spoon. Her stubborn daughter *would* take the prescribed dosage. Damned if she was going to let this hell of infected ears go on any longer than necessary.

"What's all the ruckus?"

Roni looked up to find Sam standing in the doorway, holding a tall glass of something iced and cool. He was breathtaking, his shoulders broad under his striped rodeo shirt, just a haze of golden stubble shadowing his jaw. Rested, relaxed, not a care in the world after a night of freedom—that's what his loose-hipped stance said to her in her exhaustion. And Roni couldn't have felt more put-upon and ill-used if he'd come up and kicked her.

"Where have you been?"

He lifted an eyebrow, a gesture that somehow censured her for her frowsy appearance and shrewish tone. "Trying to resurrect that engine. It's a no-go. I don't know what the hell we're going to do now."

"Yeah, well, we've all got our problems," she muttered, glaring blearily at the measurements on the spoon.

"Need some help?"

"No!" By God, this was her turf, and she was going to prove that she could handle it. Swiftly she tucked Jessie into the crook of her arm and stuffed the loaded spoon into her mouth. "There."

Jessie gulped, gasped and gagged, and her eyes got panicky when she couldn't catch her breath.

"Hey, watch it!" Sam ordered, advancing into the room.

Alarmed, Roni jerked the child upright and pounded her between the shoulder blades. Jessie promptly threw up her supper of strained carrots and peas as well as the second spoonful of pink medicine—right in the middle of the twin bed mattress.

"Holy Jehoshaphat! What are you trying to do to her?" Sam shouted.

"Don't yell at me." Roni grabbed a clean cloth diaper to dab at Jessie's chin while the child screamed out her fright. Her own lip wobbled. "I'm doing the best that I can."

"To do what? Strangle her?" Setting his glass aside, Sam picked up a towel and covered the mess on the bed.

"Don't you dare criticize me." Moisture prickled behind Roni's tired lids as she struggled to hold Jessie. "You don't know what it's like. She won't...and I tried to...and then she wouldn't..."

"Hey, get a grip, Curly." He reached out a hand.

"Easy for you to say," she half sobbed, half snarled, and jerked away. "Out gallivanting, enjoying yourself while I've been dealing with a sick child. She's still got fever, you know. And now I'm going to miss tomorrow's deadline." Hot tears trickled down her cheeks, and her voice rose on a wail. "I've *never* missed a deadline...."

"I haven't exactly been out partying," he said, defending himself.

"But you haven't been *here.*" She wiped her nose on her sleeve, and she and the baby sobbed in unison.

"Lord, you're dead on your feet, aren't you?"

"How astute of you to notice." Her voice cracked with the attempted sarcasm.

"You need some help."

She glared at him. "Bingo, cowboy."

Sam set his fists to his hips and glared back. "Then why the hell didn't you just say so? I didn't even know about your damned deadline. Am I supposed to be a mind reader or something?"

"You—you could have asked," she said, hiccuping. "But I know how busy you've been."

Sam's expression softened. "Not too busy for you. What were you trying to prove, Curly? Didn't we agree that this was going to be a mutual effort?"

Suddenly ashamed of her petulance, Roni ducked her head. "I—I'm just so tired, Sam. And I've got so much work to do."

"And you apparently don't know beans about communication, either, lady. We'll have to work on that." He lifted Jessie from her arms. The little girl magically quieted and gazed at her mother with guileless blue eyes. "But right now you're officially off duty."

"But her medicine—"

"I'll handle it." He smoothed Roni's hair back from her hot brow and kissed her forehead. "You get a shower and a nap, and then you can work on that commission, okay?"

"Uh, okay." Punch-drunk, she blinked at him. How dare he try to be nice to her! He was the most infuriating, as well as the handsomest, man she knew. But here she'd failed again, at the one task she'd set for herself. A new wave of tears threatened.

"Now don't start that again," Sam warned gently.

"I'm sorry, Sam," she said on a little painful gasp. "I thought I could do it."

"For crying out loud, Curly, even God needs a helping hand now and then. You go on. I'll hold down the fort."

"But you must be tired, too."

He gave her a lopsided grin. "It's a matter of degree, I'd say. Don't argue. *Git.*"

Roni got.

It was truly surprising what a bath, a sandwich and a brief nap could do to revive a person. When Roni entered her studio an hour later, she felt energized and even enthusiastic about producing a field of indigenous Texas wildflowers for the cover illustration. Grabbing up brushes and paints, she went to work with a will, focused so tightly, she barely heard the sounds Sam and Jessie made in the rest of the house.

When she daubed the final speck of russet into the heart of a Texas poppy and stepped back to admire the results, she was surprised to find it was well past three o'clock in the morning. But at least she'd finished. It took all she could do to lay out the shipping carton with a note asking Sam to put it in the mail the next day.

Yawning, she headed for bed, kicking off her shorts and tennis shoes just inside Jessie's door. She felt her way blindly in the darkness—and whacked her shin on the metal bed frame.

"Ouch!" Hopping, trying to suppress a whimper of pain, Roni reached for the bed and found nothing but air. Disoriented, she patted around until she found the small lamp on the bedside table and flicked it on. The soiled mattresses were missing—evidently moved out to air by Sam—and so was Jessie.

Too tired to think now, moving strictly on instinct, Roni stumbled down the hall to Sam's bedroom and peeked in. In the stream of light from the hall, she could see him sprawled out on the massive king-size bed, his bare chest and legs dark against the white sheet pulled over his middle. Miraculously, Jessie slept peacefully beside him, thumb in her mouth and bottom poked at the ceiling.

They both looked so relaxed, and the bed so delicious, Roni didn't even think. She crawled in beside her husband and daughter, gave a sigh and went right to sleep.

A cattleman's instincts usually woke him up before dawn, but as Sam surfaced from the haze of sleep, he knew that something was different this morning.

That something had warm silky skin and rounded curves and soft breasts, which at the moment were pressed against his side. Sam drew a careful breath, inhaling the fragrant scent of sleep-warmed woman, and opened one eye.

Jessie had rolled away during the night and was lodged against the headboard, snoring softly, her cheeks pink, but not the hectic fever red of the past few days. Roni, the sneak thief of sleep, lay snuggled against Sam's chest, the breath from her slightly open mouth wafting over his nipples, the hem of her cotton T-shirt shrugged up to reveal the long slender length of her legs and a glimpse of turquoise satin panties.

Sam swallowed and shut his eyes again with an inner groan. Fire stirred in his middle. It would be nothing to roll her beneath him and quench that fire once and for all. Dammit, it felt so right to hold her, as if she truly belonged in his arms. And somehow she must feel it, too, or else why would she have sought him out in her sleep?

Shifting slightly, he explored the fantasy, drifting his fingertips across the ruffled mass of her whiskey-brown curls, down her shoulder in a feather's caress, softly, softly stroking the luscious curve of female flesh. He felt like a thief himself, stealing sensations while she slept on, but he could no more refrain himself than stop the flow of the Flat Fork River.

He grazed his knuckles across the crest of her breast, watching in fascination as the nubby tip contracted, poking against the soft cotton knit with a will of its own. Almost imperceptibly, her breathing accelerated, but still she didn't stir. Emboldened, he let his palm cup the heavy weight, thinking that nothing had ever fit his hand so well.

Would they fit as well in other places? The question nearly drove him wild, and he groaned aloud.

Roni jumped, awake yet not awake, her newly acquired mother's instincts on instantaneous alert. Lifting herself with a hand splayed in the middle of his chest, she blinked owlishly at Sam. "Huh? What is it? Jessie—?"

"Shh. She's all right." His voice was husky, and he didn't dare move, for the tight bud of her nipple pressed against his palm like a burning brand. "Go back to sleep."

"Uh-huh." Happy to take the suggestion, she shifted, fitting her head into the crook of Sam's shoulder and resting her updrawn knee on his thigh with a voluptuous sigh of contentment.

Sweat popped out on the back of his neck, and he gritted his teeth with the pleasure/pain of pure arousal. But she was oblivious, unaware what her innocent embrace was doing to his overloaded circuits, and he'd be the world's worst kind of heel if he took any further advantage. After a tortuous moment, her breathing evened out again, and he gently eased her onto her back and climbed out of bed.

He was so excited, he could barely walk, and he sucked in air, willing his body into compliance. Not sparing her a look—all it would take to send him straight back to bed again—he headed for the coldest shower he could find.

Later, after Sam returned from his early-morning chores and a furious gallop on Diablo that was meant to pound the devil out of them both but hadn't, he found both his girls still fast asleep. He had no doubt it was the best thing for them, so he packed up Roni's artwork as her note requested and decided to take it on into town to the post office.

And since the transport truck wasn't good for much more than salvage now, he was going to have to lay it on the line down at the local bank, and there was no point in putting off the unpleasant task.

It was worse than unpleasant. It was downright humiliating.

"I'm sorry, Sam," Jack Phillips said as he saw Sam out of his office a couple of hours later. "The directors are adamant. Until you're able to make some payment on the principal, we just can't extend you another loan. Wish there was something more I could do."

"I appreciate it, Jack." They shook hands at the plate glass entrance. Sam started to turn away, then had a thought. "If I land that contract with Buzz Henry at the Wichita rodeo, would they consider it then?"

"Well, now, that would be different," Jack said thoughtfully. "A signed contract might shed a whole new light on the subject. Any chance of it happening?"

"Let's just say that I'm doing my damnedest," Sam drawled.

"Good luck, then. And let me know."

"Right." Nodding, Sam donned his hat and went outside. The hot May sunshine beat down on the sleepy streets of Flat Fork with the early promise of sweltering summer. The chime of the Methodist church bells sounded eleven, but only a few dusty trucks and a handful of cars moved up and down the tiny business district that hadn't changed substantially in fifty years.

The orange sign above Kelly's Pharmacy was a reminder for Sam, and he dug into his pocket for the scrap of paper with the prescription number of Jessie's medicine. Since most of the pink stuff was currently decorating the nursery's walls, he figured he might as well get the refill while he was in town. With the truck out of commission, no help at the bank and himself fresh out of ideas, it wasn't as though he had anything better to do.

The inside of the drugstore was dim and cool and smelled faintly of antiseptic. Sam approached the rear counter, coming up behind a tall cowboy dressed in an ebony shirt and jeans with his left arm in a white sling.

"You know why cowboys ride bulls, don't you, darlin'?" the cowboy was asking the pretty blonde behind the cash register.

The young woman giggled flirtatiously while she rang up his purchase—a small bottle of prescription painkillers—on the register. "No, why?"

The cowboy draped his rangy form over the counter and gave a wide grin that lifted his black mustache and made his dark eyes dance. "To meet nurses, of course."

Sam stiffened as he recognized Travis King's brash cowboy charm at work. Truth be told, it had always attracted women like flies, and it seemed things hadn't changed. Especially the fact that Travis, for all his likability and good-ole-boy charisma, was a hell-raiser and a troublemaker from the word go. And there was no getting around the fact that if he hadn't been liquored up after a big win, Kenny might still be alive today.

The girl giggled again, flirting back with the handsome cowboy. "Well, I'd say you've met your share of pretty nurses, Travis."

"Doctors, too." He winked. "You'd be surprised what a starched white coat can do to a man's imagination."

The salesgirl, who was wearing just such a jacket, blushed. Then she noticed her other customer. "Hey, Sam. What can we do for you today?"

"Missy." He tipped his straw hat and passed the prescription number to her. "A refill for Jessie."

Travis turned to the newcomer, and some of the mischief went out of his expression. "Howdy, Sam. Long time no see."

Sam barely nodded an acknowledgment. "Travis."

"Hear you got yourself hitched again. Roni Daniels, wasn't it?"

"That's right."

"You're a lucky man."

"I think so." Sam's measured gaze took in Travis's saucer-size rodeo trophy belt buckle and the white sling. "Still riding rank stock, I see."

"Yeah." He shrugged. "That's where the money is."

"Looks like you had one wreck too many."

Travis's lean features tightened at the double meaning, but he chose to ignore any intentional reference to the past, and his smile was easy as he indicated his injured arm. "This little old thing? Just a minor dust-up. I'll make the Reno rodeo in June, easy."

"Gettin' a mite old for that kind of cowboying, aren't you?"

"Naw, I'm indestructible. Too mean to quit, anyway. Besides, I got me a few Mexican Corrientes out on my place now."

Sam's attention sharpened. Corrientes cattle were the favorite rodeo roping steers. That kind of prime stock could make the difference when a rodeo supplier was talking contracts.

Travis hung a thumb in his belt loop and gave Sam a speculative look. "If I can sweet-talk Buzz Henry, maybe I can get me something going with the Wichita rodeo. Heard you're dealing with Buzz, too. Brahmas, right?"

Sam had always been a man who played his cards close to his chest, and his reply was typical. "Could be."

Travis laughed without humor. "All right, have it your way, Sam. But you and me, we could make an attractive package to offer to old Buzz. You take a notion that direction, you let me know."

*When hell freezes over.* "Sure."

At the bitter sarcasm in Sam's single-word reply, Travis's affability vanished, and his look turned hard. "You ain't ever going to let me off the hook, are you, Sam?"

Sam didn't pretend to misunderstand. "Kenny's dead."

"Hell, we weren't much more than kids. I made a mistake."

Sam's mouth tightened with anger that was still festering after more than ten years. "You sure as hell did, but don't look to me for absolution."

"As if I'd want it from a stiff-necked Preston." Travis picked up his pill bottle and stuffed it in his jeans pocket, unable to hide the stiffness of his movements, an indication that his arm wasn't his only injury. "Blame me all you want, but I've paid well for that night. I'm still paying."

Sam's only reply was a stony look. Regret and resignation flickered in Travis's dark gaze for a moment; then his mask dropped, covering whatever he was feeling with a smile that didn't reach the bleakness in his eyes. He tipped his hat at Missy behind the counter and gave Sam a brief, two-fingered salute.

"Give Roni my best, will you? I only hope the gal knows what she's in for."

Travis's parting shot ate at Sam all the way back to the ranch. *What the gal was in for?* Roni ought to know, especially since this marriage had been all her idea. But Sam's conscience besieged him as he drove down the dusty highway toward the Lazy Diamond. Roni's rough time with Jessie, his preoccupation with the ranch's troubles, maybe going flat broke with him, being groped in her sleep by a horny husband—no, she probably wasn't expecting any of that.

Sam's confidence as father, husband and breadwinner was battered, and it made his mood morose. He was a bad bargain all the way around, and if he had any sense at all, he'd try to find a way to make it up to Roni. He was supposed to be giving her time and space so she could get accustomed to living with him, then come around eventually to sharing his bed in more than just a platonic fashion, right? So he'd better not let his hormones get the better of him again as he had this morning.

For starters, he would look after Jessie this afternoon so Roni could get some more rest. Then he would get a babysitter this Friday and take his wife out to Rosie's for their usual weekend ritual. She needed a break from motherhood, and a resurrection of their previous friendly footing was bound to diffuse the volatile atmosphere. Under the circumstances, it was about the only thing he could come up with.

Feeling somewhat better for having a plan—even one so modest—Sam entered the house, only to find that the sick-room atmosphere he'd been expecting had turned magically into a bustling hive of activity. Country-western music blared from the radio, a pot of something aromatic bubbled on the stove, what appeared to be all of Jessie's nursery furniture and equipment had been transferred to the front parlor, and the faint but undeniable scent of paint permeated the air.

"Sam? Is that you?" Roni popped out of Jessie's doorway, appearing totally restored in tight jeans and sleeveless cotton top knotted at her midriff. Her eyes were bright, and a perky ponytail bobbed at the back of her head. "There you are. What took you so long? Have you eaten? I made some soup—"

"Whoa, woman." Slightly boggled, Sam walked to her and caught her by the shoulders, inspecting her closely. She had made a total transformation from the weeping wreck of the night before. "How do you feel?"

"Great." She beamed up at him. "Best night's rest I've had in years. How'd you sleep?"

"Uh…" Sam gulped, forcing back the images of a sleep-tousled female in his arms. His palms tingled on her bare skin, and it was all he could do not to pull her into himself and ravish her smiling mouth. *So much for good intentions.* With an inward groan of self-denial, he released her and cleared his throat. "I slept just fine. How's Jessie?"

"See for yourself." Roni pointed. Jessie sat in her walker, babbling to herself and swatting the tray that held an assortment of brightly colored plastic toys. "No more fever."

"Well, hallelujah for that," Sam drawled, amazed. He registered the mostly empty room, the spread newspapers, the open paint cans, and his amazement grew. "So *now* what's going on?"

"Oh, this?" Roni shrugged. "I started scrubbing the medicine off the walls, but then I figured it would be simpler to paint. Remember, I told you we'd have to do something with this room to make it special for Jessie? So why not now? What do you think about a mural?"

"A mural?" Sam blinked, knocked for a loop by this display of boundless energy from a woman he'd sworn mere hours earlier was at death's door.

"I've got the cutest idea for some Western critters," Roni enthused. "I can use trompe l'oeil to bring the outdoors inside. You don't mind, do you?"

"What? Of course not. I just don't want you knocking yourself out."

"But this is fun. And I have plenty of paint left over." She pushed Jessie's walker ahead of them with her foot and looped her arm through Sam's. "Come on, I'll fix your lunch and you can tell me how the meeting at the bank went."

"How did you know about that?" he asked sharply.

"Angel mentioned you might be going." In the kitchen, she handed Jessie a wooden spoon to play with, then reached for a soup bowl as Sam took his accustomed place at the head of the table. "How bad is the truck?"

"It was dead on arrival at Hartwell's Garage."

Accepting that, she placed the bowl of vegetable beef soup on the table with a basket of crackers. "Okay, now what?"

"Now, nothing." Hungry as he was, having to admit defeat stung his pride and stole his appetite.

"But, Sam—"

"I'm working on it, all right?" To keep from having to explain further, he picked up his spoon and began to eat.

Roni looked up from handing Jessie a cracker, taken aback by his vehemence. Sam ignored her, swallowing soup as if he were on a deadline. Roni stepped up behind his chair, and he jumped as she began to knead the tight muscles in his neck.

"Didn't you give me a lecture about communication last night?" she asked softly. "How are we going to make this work if you don't come clean with me, cowboy? Tell me what's going on."

Irritated at being backed into a corner, as well as by the way his body leapt at her soft but insistent touch, Sam threw down his spoon. "All right, you want to know the worst? Here it is."

Succinctly, he laid out the situation with the vehicle, the bank, the necessity of landing the rodeo contract to ensure the survival of the Lazy Diamond.

"I see," Roni said when he finished. "We're between a rock and a hard place."

"Yeah." Sam pushed aside his unfinished soup.

"But there's something else," she guessed. "What is it?"

"Nothing."

"Sam…" In a revival of a childhood ritual, she pinched the tendon in the curve of his neck and shoulder in warning. "Communication, remember?"

"Would you cut that out?" He caught her hand and drew her around. Obediently, she perched on the edge of the bench, knee to knee with him, but her gaze held a demand he couldn't ignore. His mouth twisted.

"All right, I saw Travis at the drugstore. Turns out he's running a few roping steers and trying to do business with Buzz Henry, too. And he had the nerve to suggest we throw in together."

"Sounds as though he was testing the waters."

"Well, he can drown in them for all I care," Sam growled.

"Think about it, Sam. It's not such a bad idea."

"What?"

Roni nodded, her expression serious. "He's raising roping cattle, and you've got riding bulls. Having a partner
would cut expenses in half. You know everything about
raising cattle, but hate the traveling and selling. We all
know Travis has never had a clue about ranching, but he's
got a line of bull that could sell an Eskimo an ice maker."

"You're crazy if you think I'd hook up with that rodeo
bum," Sam said, his face going dark as thunder. "So you
can just keep your damn-fool advice to yourself."

"You used to value my 'damn-fool advice' when I was
your drinking buddy and not just your wife," she retorted
hotly.

He groaned. "Now don't start that."

"Well, it's true. Holding a grudge against Travis all these
years about what happened to your brother is a waste of
emotional energy." Her expression softened. "You need to
let it go, Sam, for your own sake, if not for Travis's."

"Forget it. I can't."

"Then think about it this way. Can you really *afford* to
let pride make you turn down an opportunity that could
save the Lazy Diamond?"

Her question cut deep, and his jaw hardened. "I never
noticed before that you've got a real mean streak in you,
Curly."

"Then what *are* you going to do?"

"Hell, I'll figure out something." He rubbed his nape
irritably. "I suppose I could borrow Buck Dawson's hauling trailer for a couple of days next week to deliver those
three bulls to Denton."

Roni chewed her lip. "If worst came to worst, you could
sell off a parcel of land."

"That's not an option."

"Well, let me help. I've got some savings...."

"Absolutely not!" Disturbed at the implication that he couldn't support his family, Sam rose from the table.

Roni's own annoyance showed in the compression of her mouth. "Look, we're partners, aren't we? Why can't I pitch in? It's not for you or me, it's for Jessie."

"And I'd be a sorry SOB to start draining your resources the first time I hit some rough going, wouldn't I?" he returned, his voice harsh with a mixture of pricked pride and masculine defensiveness. He saw the flicker of hurt behind her eyes and made an effort to temper his flayed emotions. "Look, it's going to be all right. I'll figure something out, okay? Don't worry about it."

She opened her mouth to continue the argument, then apparently thought better of it. "All right, Sam. If you say so. Have you seen Jessie's newest trick?"

Relief that she'd dropped the subject made Sam's response almost genial. "No, what's she done now?"

Lifting the baby out of her walker, Roni popped her into Sam's waiting arms. "Come on, Jessie, show Daddy how to patty-cake."

Chortling merrily, the redheaded charmer dimpled, then clapped her plump hands together at Roni's prompting.

"Looks like we got us a prodigy, Mom," Sam said, grinning. "Say, if she's well enough, maybe we could get Krystal to keep her so we could go to Rosie's Friday night for a while."

"Why, Sam," Roni smiled warmly, "I'd love to."

He bounced the little girl slightly, evoking a squeal of delight. "And I thought maybe I could watch her this afternoon so you could take a nap or something."

Her expression softened, became almost tender. "That's very thoughtful of you, but I'm okay, really. And don't you have work to do?"

His voice was dry. "Honey, there's always work to do on a ranch."

She laughed. "I'm beginning to understand that."

"I guess I should check the water level in the north pond before we move those yearlings."

"Then I'm sure Jessie would love to go with you for the ride, and a few hours' uninterrupted time would give me a good start on her room."

"Then it's settled. Come on, Little Bit," he said, chucking Jessie under her double chin. "Want to go for a ride with Dad?"

Jessie babbled enthusiastically, making them both laugh. Sam turned toward the door, reaching for his hat on its peg.

"We'll be back after a while," he said.

"Fine. Have fun." Hands stuck in the rear pockets of her jeans, Roni followed him. "Be sure to take the diaper bag."

"Gotcha."

"And by the way, I hope you don't mind if Jessie and I bunk in with you for a couple of nights."

"Huh?" Sam's head snapped around with almost comical swiftness, and he nearly dropped the diaper bag. "In my bed, with me? Again?"

"Because of the paint smell." Roni's eyes were wide and guileless. "You wouldn't want Jessie to breathe all that, would you? It wouldn't be good for her."

"No, of course not." Sam nearly strangled on the words. But didn't Roni have any inkling what she was suggesting? How the devil was he supposed to keep his promise to himself not to rush her if she was curled up practically naked next to him all night long? Sweat popped out under his arms and his loins tightened.

She continued. "And it's useless to set up my bed again until I'm finished in there, right?"

"Uh—" She was so absolutely reasonable and unconcerned that there was no logical way for him to refute the idea. "I guess."

"Thanks, Sam." She bobbed on her toes and gave him a sisterly peck on the cheek. "I knew you'd understand."

What choice did she give him? He was trapped, with no way to avoid the pure torture of having her close and yet still untouchable. One would almost think...

He shot her a sharp, suspicious look, but her expression was perfectly innocent. No, Curly wasn't devious like other females, so he'd better not read anything into this that wasn't there. His only option was to be a good sport, and grin and bear it.

He hoped he'd survive.

# Six

The man was made of cast iron. Cold, unfeeling cast iron.

It was the only explanation, Roni decided, bending over the edge of the tub to give Jessie's yellow duck a squeeze. While Jessie splashed and squealed her delight at her morning bath time, the rubber duckie gave a dejected whistle that mirrored Roni's mood exactly. After all, she and Sam had spent four nights in the same bed, she'd worn everything from a sophisticated black satin slip to frilly baby-doll pajamas, and all the man had done was snore. Did she have to come to bed buck naked to get noticed? It was downright humiliating.

Of course, to be fair, there had been a one-year-old in the room with them, and Sam had a lot on his mind, what with the ranch's current financial pinch.

*Yeah, but he's not dead.*

Roni made a face. Maybe he just wasn't interested anymore. And, short of actually painting over everything and starting again, she'd drawn out the project in Jessie's room as long as she could. She wasn't going to be able to use that excuse to bunk with Sam much longer.

Actually, in her opinion, the mural was turning out rather well, all her frustrated energy pouring out in a creative furor that had produced a whimsical Western landscape with gnomelike gophers, playful cacti and a family of lovable coyotes. To keep Jessie entertained while she worked, Roni had made up stories about the creatures that weren't half bad. In fact, with a bit more work, there just might be a kid's picture book in the offing, and any profits could be socked away for Jessie's college fund. The idea gave Roni a lot of pleasure.

But in the meantime, her feminine self-esteem was at an all-time low. Maybe she should just tell Sam she'd changed her mind about the physical side of their marriage. But what if he turned her down? The mental picture made her cringe in hot embarrassment. She'd never be able to look him in the eye again!

No, she valued their friendship too highly to put him on the spot, but it appeared he was immune to the apparently inept subtleties of her seduction techniques. It was enough to make a woman bite nails—ten-penny ones!

"Ready to get out, honey?" Roni reached for the baby, but Jessie laughed and did a belly flop in the four inches of bathwater, a clear indication that she still wanted to play.

"Well, just a minute more, but the water is stone cold. Here, let's warm it up a little."

She twisted the hot water knob, finding it stubborn, as usual—then suddenly everything happened at once. The entire knob assembly gave way in her hand and hot water spewed out of the wall pipe. Scalding liquid splashed her arm and she screamed, not so much out of her own pain, but out of terror for Jessie. Desperately, she grabbed the baby, pulling her out of the tub and away from the dangerous flood. Jessie gave a horrifying howl that chilled Roni's core.

"Oh, God—Jessie!"

Sam burst through the bathroom door, still clutching his morning coffee mug. "What? What the hell's wrong?"

Her face white, Roni frantically examined Jessie's tender skin for burns. Thankfully, no blisters or red marks marred her translucent redhead's hide.

"She's all right," Roni said, her relief vast and dizzying. She cuddled the screaming, wet child to her breast, not caring that her silk robe, now soaked, clung to her, as revealing as a second skin. "Just scared. The water—turn it off! Where's the cutoff valve?"

Sam look around, befuddled. "Uh—it's an old setup. There may not be one. I'll have to turn it off at the pump."

As Roni's own fear abated, it was replaced by a fury that was as scalding as the water still pouring from the wall. "Well, that's just great. No water at all now. Didn't I ask you to fix this thing?"

"I was getting to it...."

"Getting to it!" Roni shrieked. "Your daughter could have been badly burned! Don't you even care?"

Sam was dumbstruck. "Now wait a minute, Curly! Of course I care."

"Well, you sure have a way of showing it." She was crying, the emotional floodgates opened by shock and fright and pure frustration. "I told you this could happen. But no, you're so busy fiddling with your damn cows, you can't even take care of your wife's and daughter's most basic needs. This whole house is falling apart around our ears and you aren't concerned in the least."

"If I don't *fiddle* with those damn cows, we can't afford to fix anything," he said in a tight voice.

Roni whipped a towel from the rack and wrapped Jessie in it. "Well, if you weren't so filled with stubborn pride, you could find a way."

"There are more important things than money." His voice turned bitter. "I thought you knew that, but maybe you're more like Shelly about the subject than I supposed."

She sucked in a breath that was pure pain. Blood drained from her face, leaving her pale as milk, but her eyes were flames.

"You bastard," she whispered. Lip trembling, head high, she stalked past him.

"Oh, hell, Roni!" Sam caught her arm, and she gave a gasp of pain. Scowling, he pulled up the sleeve of her robe, revealing an ugly red splotch on her forearm just forming blisters. Air rushed between his teeth in an angry hiss. "Why didn't you tell me you were hurt?"

She jerked free, glaring at him with haughty dignity through lashes spiky with tears. "I can take care of myself. I've been doing it a long time."

Sam's jaw worked with tension. "I'll get the first-aid spray—"

"You just figure out a way to turn off that water before it floods the entire house," she snapped. "I'm going to dress Jessie before she gets sick again."

*No thanks to you.*

The words hung in the air, as palpable as though she had spoken them aloud.

Reaching under the torrent, he pulled the tub's drain plug. "Fine. Suit yourself."

"Thank you, I will." Roni stormed past him.

She heard him slam out of the house moments later. Before she finished dressing Jessie, the gurgle of the water cutoff echoed from the pipes all over the house, and then she heard the ill-tempered sound of Sam's truck spewing gravel as he peeled out of the driveway.

Fine. She didn't want his sorry company anyway, not after the things he'd said. Roni wiped away a new stream of tears, then sniffed in determination.

Someone had to take care of things, and it looked as though that someone was her. Buttoning Jessie's playsuit, she pressed a kiss on her daughter's damp russet curls.

"Come on, sweetie. Mommy's got some work to do."

He owed her an apology.

Some men would bring roses as a peace offering, but Sam had something better. He glanced at the sack marked with a prominent hardware store logo that sat on the truck seat beside him. Plumbing parts might not be the most romantic gift in the world, but he was sure Roni would appreciate the practicality as well as the symbolism. And maybe it would get him out of the doghouse at the same time.

A glance at the angle of the sun and the empty rumble of his belly told him it was long past noon. It was probably just as well that it had taken him and Angel longer than expected to pick up Buck Dawson's trailer. After the morning's explosion, he and Roni both needed some time to cool off.

It was the heat, that was all, he told himself. That's why they'd blown up like a thunderstorm over a near accident that should have left them clinging together in thanksgiving instead of yelling things at each other they didn't mean.

*Yeah, sure.*

It was heat all right, Sam acknowledged. A pure sexual heat, a hunger that gnawed at him, made him crazy, kept him from concentrating on more important things—like how to keep the Lazy Diamond afloat. You couldn't sleep in the same bed with a woman, smell her unique perfume night after night, hear the soft sounds she made when she dreamed and not go a little mad. Something had to give— and soon. He only hoped it wasn't his sanity.

There was a white van parked in the yard when Sam drove up. And men climbing up and down his porch steps. And a stained bathtub perched like a beached whale atop a pile of debris in his yard.

"What the hell—?" Climbing out of his truck with his sack of supplies, he paused long enough to read the lettering on the side of the van. Cutler's Plumbing/No Job Too Big Or Too Small.

The pulse in his temple pounded, and he scowled. Damn her. He met Steve Cutler coming out the door.

"Hey, Sam. Look, don't worry about the mess. We'll haul everything off when we finish, okay?"

Ever cheerful, Steve clapped Sam on the back and went off whistling toward the van, not even noticing Sam's lack of response.

Inside, the activity and noise were deafening. Sam found Roni standing in the parlor with Jessie on her hip, happily watching the demolition of the bathroom and the kitchen. She didn't even realize he was home until he touched her shoulder and she jumped.

"What the devil is this?" he growled.

She tilted her chin, her expression belligerent. "What's it look like? They're replumbing the house."

Fury darkened Sam's features, and his voice was low and dangerous. "I can't pay for this."

"*I* can." She turned back to watch the bustle. "Consider it a wedding present."

Her contemptuous words slammed into his solar plexus, tore through his gut, emasculated him. Only a woman could zero in on a man's most vulnerable spot and then flay it unmercifully. Somehow, he'd thought Curly was different. Now he knew he'd been wrong, but he would be damned if he would show her the power she had to hurt him.

"Tell them to stop," he ordered hoarsely.

"No."

"Then *I* will."

She caught his wrist, and her fingers, though slender, artistic and very feminine, had a grip like steel. "I said *no*. You accuse me of being a grasping bitch like Shelly, but I'm giving you—us—something we need. Aren't you man enough to accept the gift?"

He looked at her hard. Pulling free of her grasp, he dropped the hardware bag at her feet. "I guess not."

Turning on his heel, he stomped out of the house, ignoring her when she called his name.

He didn't stop when he got to the barn, didn't stop as he saddled Diablo, didn't stop as he galloped over Lazy Diamond land that, for the time being at least, was still his. It seemed to him in that moment that he had very little else.

After an hour, he found himself negotiating the little hillock that bounded the stock pond on the north section. He didn't recall much of his route, but Diablo was blowing and they were both tired, so it seemed as good a place as any to rest until his thoughts and his pride reestablished themselves into some sort of order. It was pretty here, with a shady stand of young willows on one side and a lush meadow of grass, still green and unwilted by the late-spring dryness. The group of cream-colored Brahma yearlings his crew had moved in earlier in the week dotted a tree-lined rise in the distance.

Dismounting, Sam let Diablo drink, then threw himself down on the embankment and stared at the water while the animal grazed. After a while, the horse pricked his ears and Sam roused enough to stand to meet the intruder.

It was Roni under that Western hat, sitting tall on a sorrel mare, with Jessie peeping over her shoulder from a perch in an aluminum-framed backpack. Roni's pert backside was encased in tight jeans that accentuated every curve, and the backpack harness stretched her red cotton shirt over her full breasts in a manner that left nothing to the imagination.

Hiding his surprise that she'd followed him, he watched her approach, his features stony. There was no way on God's green earth he was going to continue the conflict, not while his anger and chagrin were still simmering so close to the surface. But damn Curly, anyway. It looked as though she wasn't giving him much choice. Crossing his arms over his chest, he set his jaw and waited for her.

Roni reined the mare to a halt beside Sam. Though her expression was calm, there was uncertainty behind her dark eyes.

"Go home," he said.

A sultry wind loosed a tendril of dark hair from the clip at her nape and blew it across her lips. With exaggerated care, she drew it free from the corner of her mouth with a fingertip and lifted her chin. "No. And don't just stand there, help me with Jessie. She weighs a ton."

Before he could protest, she was shrugging out of the backpack, and he had no choice but to take the contraption or risk Jessie falling. Holding a child who smiled at him in delighted recognition from beneath a pretty bonnet certainly made it hard to remember why he was mad, but Sam felt obligated to make another attempt.

"I'm not in the mood for this, Curly."

"Tough." Dismounting, she dragged a bulging sack off the saddle horn. She chose a shady spot, spread a tablecloth, pulled off her hat and plopped down on her knees. "Have a seat. It's lunchtime."

Bewildered, Sam stared as she unloaded her sack of goodies, spreading out an assortment of fruit, sandwiches and cookies. *A picnic?* After what had just happened between them, she wanted to have a gol-danged picnic?

She pulled out two plastic cups and a bottle of champagne that had been sitting in the refrigerator since the wedding. "Let's drink this while it's still cool."

"Are we celebrating something?" he growled, standoffish and suspicious.

A small "pop" sounded as she released the cork, and she raised the bottle in a mock salute. "Insanity, I think. Sit. I'm starved."

Jessie spotted the cookies at that point, so Sam had to lift her out of the carrier and set her down to play on the cloth. He stretched his own length out beside the child as she chortled and cooed and tried to catch blades of grass in her chubby fists.

"Here." Roni passed him a cup of champagne. "And try to remember it's not the usual rotgut you drink."

"Thank you for the warning."

It set his teeth on edge, knowing that she'd lived a champagne kind of life out there in California with the film industry hoi polloi, knowing that he came across as some kind of bad-tempered Texas hayseed by comparison. Feeling mutinous and resentful, he took a gulp, swishing the sparkling wine around his teeth, letting the bubbles fill his sinuses, generally making as obnoxious a process of it as he could. Roni watched him over the edge of her own cup, a small frown pleating her brow, but then something dissolved in her expression and she laughed helplessly.

"What's so funny?" he demanded, heat rising in his cheeks.

"You and me." She toasted him broadly, then tilted her cup and drained the contents.

"Hey, watch it."

"Why?" She blinked at him, her eyes slightly unfocused. "Afraid I'll get drunk and say something stupid? I've already proven I don't need Dutch courage for that."

"What's that supposed to mean?"

"I'm trying to apologize, you lunkheaded cowboy." Her color was too high, and she buried her face in her hands with a groan. "And there I go again. I'm sorry, Sam. I don't know what's the matter with me lately. I didn't mean to say those ugly things. I never wanted to hurt you."

Sam's throat constricted, and he reached out to lift her chin so he could see her face. "Me, neither."

"I was just so furious," she added in a rush. "I wasn't thinking about how you'd feel when I called Steve Cutler. I realize I should have discussed it with you, but dammit, Sam, you won't let me do anything."

"Huh? How can you say that?" He frowned, mystified, and his fingertips lingered, stroking the soft underside of her chin, satiny-smooth and faintly damp with perspiration. "You're just about killing yourself talking care of Jessie and the house and me and your commissions. You're doing plenty—too damn much, the way I see it."

She pulled back, shaking her head in frustration. "I mean you won't let me get close. You won't talk to me about your problems unless I push my way in. And you won't let me help, when I'm ready, willing and able to do so."

"There are some things a man has to do by himself."

"I've had it up to *here* with your macho bull." She clenched her fist in his chambray shirt and shook him. "Listen here, buddy, I'm a partner in this thing, same as you. That's why I called the plumber. And we *are* getting new pipes in that house, and I *will* pay for it, so you better get used to the idea."

"Jeez, Curly," he drawled, "why didn't you just tell me how you really felt?"

"Aww...men!" She thrust him away, then grabbed Jessie who was chewing a mouthful of grass. "Oh, eat your sandwich."

Sam couldn't prevent a smile. "Curly, you're a maniac."

She bounced Jessie on her leg and gave him a suspicious look. "Does that mean you're going to forgive me?"

"Only if it works both ways." He shifted uncomfortably and began to unwrap a ham sandwich, not meeting her eyes. "I—uh, that is... Look, you're nothing like Shelly and I was way out of line, so if you can just forget it, let's call a truce, okay?"

"Yes." She gave a sigh of relief. "I'd like that. I get all knotted up inside when we argue."

"Me, too." He caught her wrist, turning it to inspect the scald. "So, how's the arm?"

"Not bad. I put some salve on it. Let's just put it behind us, okay?" She beamed at him. "Have some more champagne. Have some strawberries."

Sam was more than willing. Giving her a half smile, he polished off his sandwich and accepted the cup she refilled for him, along with a handful of succulent berries. "Kind of fancy vittles for a cowpuncher's picnic."

"A peacekeeping expedition of this proportion demanded extraordinary measures."

A reluctant grin tilted his mouth. "Well, ma'am, I guess it worked at that."

Laughing, she bit into a strawberry while helping Jessie drink juice from a two-handled baby cup. Finished, the child gave a sigh and curled up next to Sam's outstretched leg, murmuring sleepily to herself. "Gosh, she's tired."

"Didn't she get her nap?"

Roni shook her head, lowering her voice as she rubbed the baby's back in a soothing rhythm. Jessie's eyelids fluttered once, twice; then she settled into sleep. "It's a bit noisy at the house right now."

"I can imagine," Sam said dryly.

Roni's warm brown gaze flickered to his face, then away, as though she were unwilling to risk another confrontation on that issue. Well, the deed was done, Sam thought. No use fighting about a bunch of pipes and faucets any further. But he would find a way to pay Steve Cutler for his services at some point. To keep the peace, it wouldn't hurt to let think Roni she'd gotten her way. *This time.*

Roni poured herself more champagne, sipping and dipping strawberries into the bubbly liquid as her gaze roamed the lush landscape and the sun-dappled surface of the large pond.

"It's nice and quiet here," she said. "We used to come here a lot, didn't we? I'd forgotten how pretty it is."

"Beautiful."

But Sam wasn't looking at the scenery. It was Roni's mouth, slick and rosily stained with berry juice, that snared his attention. He was amazed that he could run the emotional gamut from crazed fury to gut-clenching lust in just a few short moments. It was pretty clear that ole Sam was losing his ever-lovin' mind.

"It's awfully hot already for May, though," Roni was saying.

She plucked open the top button of her blouse, lifting the fabric to encourage any wayward breeze. Sam swallowed hard as a trickle of moisture slipped from the base of her throat and disappeared into the mysterious hollows of her cleavage.

"Yeah, hot," Sam said hoarsely. "And it's going to get worse."

"Don't say that. I'm about to melt right now as it is, and this stuff is making me muzzy-headed." She drained her cup anyway, then unclipped her hair and lifted it off her neck. Her eyes strayed to the pond, cool and green and inviting. "Sam?"

The sight of her breasts pressing against the fabric of her shirt robbed him of speech. "Hmm?"

"Remember how we all used to sneak up here when we were kids? You and Kenny and me? Even Travis sometimes."

"Uh-huh."

"Remember what we did?"

How could he forget? Skinny-dipping with the gang, a forbidden pleasure, all childish innocence and fun. "I remember—what are you doing?"

Without looking at him, she rapidly tugged off her boots and socks, then stood, swaying rather dizzily as she unsnapped her jeans and began to shuck them off. "What's it look like?"

A bolt of sizzling alarm shot from Sam's skull to the soles of his feet. "Veronica Jean!"

"Watch Jessie for me while I cool off, okay?"

Dropping her jeans, she walked toward the water's edge, unbuttoning her shirt and then dropping that in the grass, too, apparently oblivious to the fact that neither she nor Sam was ten years old anymore.

It was that damned red silk lingerie again! Sam's body leapt to life, and he groaned at the sight of full breasts cupped by sheer scarlet net, slender hips caressed by the briefest scrap of vermillion lace. Then she was wading into the water, taking hedonistic pleasure in the sensuality of cool liquid on heated flesh. She eased under, making soft sounds of delight reminiscent of a woman in the heights of passion, then swam a few yards out.

Sam watched, mesmerized and helpless. When she stood up again, she lifted her face to the sun and pushed back her streaming hair. Water sluiced off her, turning her garments transparent, and Sam thought the top of his head would pop off.

With a glance to ensure that Jessie was still soundly asleep on the cloth, he eased painfully to his feet and stormed to the water's edge. Unfulfilled lust lashed at him, made him angry in a way that couldn't even compare to his earlier rage.

Did Roni think he was made of iron? That his willpower was inexhaustible? Surely it was the champagne that made her so foolhardy. Whatever the reason, he was at his limit, and the torture had to end.

"Curly, get your butt out of there right now!"

She spun to face him, the water lapping at her thighs. She blinked, her annoyance at his preemptory tone clear, and then something indefinable changed. Tilting her head, she pursed her lips and looked at him through her lashes, feline and taunting and provocative. "Make me."

He saw red.

Red silk. Ripe, berry-red lips. A rosy blush of satin skin and female flesh.

Engulfed in the scarlet flames of passion, he stepped into the water. Her eyes widened as he took another step, filling his boots, saturating his jeans.

Roni stumbled back, but it was too late. Hooking an arm around her waist, Sam jerked her close. The breath left her with a whoosh as she landed against his rock-hard chest, then felt another part of him equally rigid. He threaded his other hand through her wet hair, tilting her head back at a painful angle, holding her still as he breathed fire across her face.

"You're driving me insane. Why?" he demanded, his voice harsh.

She trembled. "I don't know."

He slid his fingers beneath the elastic band of her bikini panties, pressing into the small of her back so that she made an intimate acquaintance with the bulge in the front of his jeans. "Don't you know what you're asking for?"

"Maybe I do." She licked her lips and tried to smile, but the soft mounds of her breasts were crushed against his shirt and her breathing was ragged.

"Don't fancy it up in your mind," he said, making his words brutally honest. "It's release, pure and simple. For both of us."

"You're so sure," she said, gasping.

"I'm a man. You're a woman. We're in the same house, the same damn bed. Forget that crock about a platonic relationship. It isn't working, at least for me."

"Sam, I—"

"Just be quiet." He covered her mouth with a blistering kiss. When he lifted his head, she was limp.

Breathing gustily, he half dragged, half carried her to the bank, then pressed her down into the soft grass. With one knee insinuated aggressively between her thighs, he held her face between his palms, speaking plainly, with no apologies.

"I can't think or work. Half the time, I can't decide whether to bed you or strangle you. Hell, it's a wonder we haven't killed each other."

She touched his waist. "I know. I'm sorry—"

He grimaced. "No, I'm sorry. I tried to give you time, but I've reached my limit. Given the situation, it had to happen sooner or later. And by God, it has to be sooner to save my sanity. We are going to consummate this marriage, Veronica Jean."

She quivered. "We are?"

He steeled himself against the vulnerable tremor in her voice. "Yes. You are going to share my bed, and we are going to give each other what we need to take the edge off and get back to a normal life. We talked about how this might happen. I'm sorry if you don't like it, if you're not ready, but there it is. So what have you got to say?"

She sighed and pulled his face to hers. *"Finally."*

Shock froze Sam for a timeless instant as her lips nibbled his; then the heat of realization sparked the roiling inferno inside him into a full-fledged conflagration. He covered her completely with his body, pressing her into the lush, sweet-smelling grasses, cursing the barriers of clothing that separated them. Her mouth was sweet and responsive and willing, eagerly opening for the penetration of his tongue.

With a groan, he rolled over, pulling her on top of him, rolling his thumbs in the hollows of her hipbones. She gasped, arching away from his mouth, and he raised his head to lick at the pebbled nipple poking against the wet, lacy barrier of her scarlet bra.

"Sam—oh!" Face flushed, she clutched at his shoulders. "We've got to stop."

Groaning, he bit lightly at the swell of her breast spilling out of its lacy covering. "Lady, you started this."

"We can't do it here. Not now." Her voice was rather desperate.

"Why the hell not?"

"Anyone could come up. And Jessie's awake."

For a second, he almost didn't care, but then responsibility reaffirmed itself. With another groan of pure defeated frustration, he let go of Roni. She rolled off him, her eyes wide with what he hoped was regret—or was it relief?—and scrambled toward the cloth where Jessie was rousing.

For a long moment, all Sam could do was lie on his back and stare up at the blue sky while his body throbbed in protest. Finally he came to his feet and squished in his sodden boots to gather Roni's jeans and shirt. She was kneeling, changing Jessie's diaper when he squatted down and dropped her clothes beside her.

"You'd better put these on."

"Yes." Her cheeks were still flushed and she didn't look at him.

"I guess parents have to get accustomed to this kind of interruption."

"I guess so."

"Don't think this lets you off the hook, though."

That snapped her head around. "I—I don't."

Sam touched her hair, brushing the damp, curling mass over her shoulder. "You and me, tonight. After the whippersnapper goes to bed. We have some business to finish."

She swallowed. "I know."

"We agree it's for the best."

"Yes."

"Tonight, then."

She nodded. "Tonight."

So they made the date. But as they rode home toward the ranch house, Sam had to wonder why the woman who'd agreed to become his lover and wife in fact looked as though she were riding to her own execution.

# Seven

"She's asleep?"

"Uh-huh." Roni stood in the bedroom doorway, looking back over her shoulder toward Jessie's room. The pale beam of a night-light was the only illumination in the house, the low thrum of the air conditioner the only sound besides the nervous pounding of her heart. "I've never been this far away from her at night. What if I don't hear her?"

"You'll hear her." Sam's disembodied voice came from the darkened depths of the bedroom.

"But—"

"Curly, I thought we'd agreed."

Roni shivered under her simple emerald gown, and her voice was small. "We did."

There came a rustle of sheets being pulled back. "Then come here."

Roni swallowed, and slowly stepped across the carpet toward a man whose shadowy form she felt more than saw.

How could she want this so badly, and yet feel so afraid? She reached the edge of the bed, then jumped when a warm hand closed around her wrist. Gently Sam pulled her down beside him. She lay on her back, tension stretching every cord and tendon, waiting, waiting. She could smell the menthol of his shaving cream and the musk of his skin, but with him propped on his elbow, all she could see of Sam's face was a shaded outline, and he seemed a stranger to her.

"I won't hurt you," he said at last.

Her breath, which she hadn't even been aware she was holding, left her in a little rush. "I know that."

"Then why...?" He slid a hand to her waist, rubbing his callused fingers soothingly over the cool silk of her garment. "You're stiff as a firepoker. Do I frighten you that much?"

She gulped, all her fears crowding her thoughts. It was all so cold-blooded. What if she couldn't please him? She wasn't that experienced, really. What did he expect of a lover? Oh, Lord, how was she going to go through with this?

She forced panic back and spoke quietly. "I'm sorry. It's a big step, that's all."

Disappointment colored his voice. "Curly, if you're not ready—"

"No—I mean, yes, I am." Heat stained her cheeks, but she resolutely covered his questing hand with her own and drew it to her breast. "I'm just a little nervous. It'll be all right."

But it seemed he hardly heard her, suddenly fascinated with the heavy weight of her breast in his palm, his thumb exploring the sensitive tip. Dipping his head, he sought her mouth, and Sam, who had always been assured and graceful to her, now moved awkwardly, bumping noses before finding her lips.

His kiss was too gentle, over too quickly for Roni, and then he was stripping off her gown. Finding her nude beneath it, he pulled her against his body, and she gasped at the rich, dark, hair-dusted warmth of his own nakedness, blatantly masculine and intimidating. His turgid sex pressed against her thigh, branding her with his right of possession.

"Relax, Curly." Sam's voice held the rasp of growing passion. "Everything's going to be okay, I promise."

She tried. She really did.

But whether from nerves or inexperience or ineptitude, she couldn't fully respond to his kisses and caresses. In his consideration for her nervousness, he held her like a china doll when what she needed was his masculine power to overcome her anxiety. His touch, though gentle, was too polite, too well mannered to push her into full arousal, and she fell short of the plateaus that would have led her to forgetfulness time and again. She allowed him every liberty, and tried to touch him, to pleasure him in return, but she was out of pace with Sam's growing urgency, and she sensed his impatience as well as his determination to make things good for her. But it was impossible, and after a while her only goal was to have him finish things.

"Now," she urged, tugging at his hips.

He slipped a finger between her legs, making her jump.

"It's okay." She touched him intimately, knowing he was drawing close to the end of his willpower. "Please, Sam, now."

Bending her knees up, he positioned himself and entered her. She gasped at the sharp pinch of discomfort.

"I'm sorry, I'm sorry." He murmured against her neck, his entire body quivering with the effort it took to hold himself still while she tried to accommodate him.

"Go ahead," she whispered, stroking his back, willing him to take his pleasure since her own was forfeit.

But when he began to move, her tension made him uncomfortable, hampering his own release and thus prolonging her distress. When he finally collapsed on top of her, they were both drenched in sweat, and Roni couldn't prevent the tears that had gathered at the corners of her eyes from sliding to her temples.

He withdrew quickly. "Aw, hell, Roni, you didn't... Here, let me help." He stroked her between her legs.

"No!" She caught his hand, staying him. "That's not necessary."

"Oh." Even in the dark, she could sense the fiery chagrin in his expression.

Roni shut her eyes miserably, knowing that she'd truly offended him by her involuntary rejection. "I—I'm a little tender right now. Could—could you just hold me awhile?"

"Sure." His voice was stiff, but his arms were sure, cuddling her spoon-fashion. The kiss he pressed to the curve of her neck seemed more than she deserved after such a disaster.

"I'm sorry," she whispered, her voice an ache.

His arms tightened around her. "Cut it out, Curly. I'm the one who let you down."

"No, it was me—"

"Look, we're not kids. You and I understand this kind of thing gets better with practice. We both wanted to know, and now we do. The worst is over, and we survived. Now get some sleep."

"Yes, Sam."

There was some comfort in his arms, but his brusque and businesslike dismissal of their earth-shattering experience chilled her. The intimacy she'd hoped for was missing, and she felt empty, cheated somehow, and that was a sharper disappointment than her failure to achieve the ultimate climactic peak. Was this all that a marriage between friends was destined to be?

In her raw and confused emotional state sleep evaded her, and when she finally slept, her dreams were fitful. She roused in the wee hours to find Sam standing naked before the window, gazing out over his rangelands. She rolled over, feigning sleep, her soul shriveling at the bitter regret in his single, softly spoken utterance.

*"Damn."*

It was a mistake, pure and simple, and Roni knew it. She and Sam had crossed a line they had no business crossing, and now things were awkward and horrible and worse than ever. And she had no idea how to fix it.

"Roni, are you listening to me?"

Roni turned away from the kitchen window and her studied perusal of the trio of miniature ruby-throated dive bombers hurtling past Krystal's cherry-red hummingbird feeder at the speed of light. "Sure I am. What did you say?"

"I asked if you wanted more coffee. Man, you're out in left field this morning." Krystal refilled Roni's mug without waiting for an answer, tilting her blond head and giving her friend a close look. "Is everything all right?"

"Of course it is." Roni took the cup and sipped coffee she didn't want, automatically checking Jessie's progress through a pile of toys situated in the middle of Krystal's comfortably furnished den. "Why shouldn't it be?"

"Then you've got your head in the clouds today because things are going so well between you and Sam?"

Roni forced a tight smile. "I guess that's it."

"Yeah, and I've got a bridge in Brooklyn I'd like to sell you." Clad in shorts and sandals, Krystal shooed Roni toward the sofa and plopped down on the other end. "Come on, the boys will be out of school for the summer in a day or two, and I won't have time to play Mother Confessor, so spit it out."

"Really, Krys." Roni laughed as she settled Indian-fashion on the couch, tucking up the gauzy crinkle skirt that matched her orange tank top. She'd pulled her hair into a French braid, and Shoshone dream catcher earrings dangled to her shoulders. "I don't know what you mean."

"What are you fighting about? Religion? Money?"

"We're not fighting."

"Then it must be about sex."

Roni felt her face go crimson. "Krystal!"

"That's it, isn't it?" Triumph sparkled in her mischievous expression. "Hooee. That's a good one. What? Does he want you to swing naked from the chandelier?"

Roni buried her face in her hand. "I don't know why I try to have an intelligent conversation with you. And we don't even have a chandelier."

Krystal made a negligent gesture. "A minor detail. All right, sister, spill it."

Roni gave an inward groan. How could she tell Krystal that her husband equated their first and only sexual encounter as "the worst?" That on arising from the bed in which they'd finally consummated their marriage, they could barely stand to look at each other, so great was their mutual embarrassment. That Sam had been in such a hurry to get away from her, he'd hightailed it out at the crack of dawn to deliver his bulls without even breakfast. And Roni was so chagrined, the thought of staying in the house while Steve Cutler's crew finished their work had just been too much, so she'd run like a coward to hide out at Krystal's. Uh-uh. Some things were just too humiliating to share.

But Krystal would wart Roni unmercifully unless she got some answers. Roni decided a diversionary tactic was in order. She set her cup aside. "Since you must know, we had a bit of a disagreement about my paying for the plumbing."

"Aha, I see. Got him in the wallet. Men can be so stupid about money."

"Isn't that the truth?" Roni sighed. Jessie crawled to the sofa, pulling up on the edge and demanding attention. Lifting her daughter up beside her, Roni handed the child one of the boy's plastic trucks to examine. "I hurt his pride, I guess, but I'm living in that house, and I had the funds to spend, so—"

"Makes no never-you-mind," Krystal said with a shake of her head. "Man like Sam Preston, you're practically attacking his manhood to offer him financial help."

"He's stubborn about it, all right." Roni's mouth drooped. "The big truck rig died for good, and things are really tight right now."

"How bad is it?"

"Bad enough that Sam's afraid if he doesn't land that rodeo contact with Buzz Henry, the Lazy Diamond may not make it."

Krystal frowned. "Gosh, I'm sorry to hear that! But he's got assets. He could sell off some of his stock, or a parcel of land, couldn't he?"

"It would just about kill him, I think."

Krystal let her head drop onto the back of the sofa and groaned. "Oh, these male egos."

"You said it. He had the opportunity to go in with Travis King, which would give him a better chance of landing the contract, but he wouldn't even consider it."

"Wouldn't be such a bad deal for Travis, either," Krystal commented, reaching over to give Jessie's tummy a quick tickle and eliciting a giggle from the baby. "From what Bud says, he'd better get out of rodeoing before it kills him."

"I wish there was some way I could convince Sam to give it a try," Roni said.

Krystal twinkled at her. "There's always that chandelier."

Roni burst out laughing just as the phone rang. Grinning, Krystal went to answer it. Jessie gave her new mother a curious look, then clapped her hands and laughed, too.

But Roni's chuckles at Krystal's ribald suggestion contained a note of ironic pain. Krystal might think Roni had some influence over Sam in the bedroom department, but Roni knew better, and the blow to her own feminine ego was devastating. How could she face Sam again? Would he expect them to go back to the way it had been? She couldn't blame him in the least. Mortification made her feel like running away, but the little girl drooling all over a truck wheel was a firm reminder of where her duty lay.

"Yes, she's here." Krystal's voice carried from the phone in the kitchen. "What? Yes, I'll tell her."

Krystal's expression as she hurried back into the den shot a bolt of alarm straight up Roni's spine. "What's the matter? Who was it?"

"Angel." Krystal plucked Jessie up and cuddled her protectively. "You've got to get to the emergency room right away. Sam's been hurt."

"Ouch!"

"Don't give me that." Dr. Hazelton tied another knot in the line of stitches across Sam's shoulder blade. "I shot you so full of Xylocaine, I know you can't feel a thing."

"That's what you think." Lying facedown on the emergency room gurney, Sam grimaced, instantly regretting it as the swelling on the side of his face protested. The tattered remnants of his blood-stained work shirt lay draped over the end of the gurney.

"Just hold still," the doctor ordered, reaching for the scissors his nurse held. "I'm nearly finished."

Sam subsided, gnashing his teeth and cursing under his breath. His whole world was going to hell in a handbasket, and now this had to happen! It was his own blamed fault, though, woolgathering about Roni when he should have been paying attention to a ton and a half of bad-tempered beef on the hoof. It could have been a lot worse than being slammed into the side of a catch pen and hooked by the tip of a horn as he dodged. Served him right for being such a fool.

He still couldn't believe the fiasco he'd made bedding his own wife. While he'd never claimed to be the best lover in the world, he'd had few complaints... until last night. Not that Roni had complained, or even resisted. No, she'd been generous and sweet and trying oh so hard, and all he'd done for her was make her cry. Sam groaned at the memory.

"You aren't getting any sympathy from me with this act," Dr. Hazelton assured him.

"Aren't you done yet, you old quack?"

"I'd watch my mouth if I were you, sonny." The physician snipped the final knot. "There you go, and as fine a piece of needlework as you're ever going to see, too. Don't even expect it to leave a scar on that tough hide of yours, which ought to please your pretty wife."

"Thanks, Doc. No offense," Sam grunted.

"None taken, son." The doctor waved to the nurse. "You can put the dressing on for me, Audrey."

The gray-haired nurse nodded cheerfully. "Sure thing, Doc."

"Where is he? Let me see him!" The door flew open, and Roni stumbled into the room in a swish of Gypsy skirts, the light in her eyes wild. She was followed by the stocky figure of Angel Morales, his straw hat clenched in his thick hands. At the sight of the crimson-drenched shirt, the raw stitches, Sam's prone figure and puffy, soon-to-be black eye, Roni froze, horror washing the color from her cheeks. "Oh my God."

"Now, it's not as bad as it looks, Veronica," Dr. Hazelton said hastily.

"Oh my God!" she repeated.

"Curly, I'm all right." Wincing, Sam levered himself to a seated position.

"What did they do to you?" she asked in a thin voice, then swayed so violently, everyone in the room jumped to keep her from falling. Pandemonium reigned for a few seconds as the nurse pushed a stool under her and the doctor forced her head between her knees.

"Breathe through your nose, Veronica. You'll be fine." Dr. Hazelton looked up at Sam with a wry twinkle behind his glasses. "Light-headed, huh? You got this gal in the family way already, my friend?"

Bending helplessly over his wife, Sam felt his face heat. "Uh—"

"No!" Roni's voice was muffled by her skirts. She sat up, breathing shallowly. "That's not it. I'll be all right in a minute. It was just the shock."

"That old bull just banged him up a bit, honey," the doctor reassured her. "Measly seven stitches. Hardly worth all the fuss."

Sam shot his middle-aged foreman a hard look. "I told Angel not to bother you."

With a half-apologetic grin creasing his swarthy face, Angel shrugged off Sam's displeasure, but Roni stiffened, the wildness flaring in her eyes again and her voice rising.

"And why shouldn't he have called me? I'm your *wife*."

After what had happened between them, Sam didn't know how to take that statement. Luckily, Dr. Hazelton filled the void.

"And you're just the one to take this man home and see that he gets a little T.L.C. for the rest of the day," he said heartily. "Audrey?"

The nurse tugged Sam back to the gurney and swiftly applied the bandages. Sam's expression was mulish.

"I've got too much to do—ow!" He glared as the doctor withdrew a hypodermic needle from his arm. "What the hell was that for?"

"Tetanus. And a little something to take the edge off. You're going to start hurting like the devil pretty soon." Dr. Hazelton handed Roni several sample bottles. "Give him a couple of these for pain. Make him rest and drink plenty of fluids. He lost a good bit of blood."

She picked up the torn, bloody shirt, her fingers working in the fabric, but her skin was no longer as pasty, and she looked more herself. "Yes, Doc."

Irritated, embarrassed, Sam clenched his jaw and stood. "I don't have time for this."

"Shut up, Sam." Roni took his arm, and her expression brooked no opposition. "For once in your life, you're going to do exactly as you're told."

Roni poured grain into Diablo's feed bin, stroked the stallion's nose, then turned on the spigot to fill the bathtub-size galvanized water trough. As the water poured out of the faucet, she perched her arms on the top boards of the corral and propped her chin on them, watching the sunset explode into a panorama of tangerine and gold.

She'd been on autopilot since getting the phone call from Angel, arranging for Krystal to keep Jessie for the night, hurrying to the hospital and then driving her very ill-tempered patient home. The injection Dr. Hazelton had given Sam had made him drowsy, and he'd slept away the afternoon, which was just as well, considering his grumpiness, Roni reflected. Angel and the crew were off finishing the delivery of the other bulls, and the barn and yards were deserted.

At least the plumbers had finished. Cleaning up after them had kept her busy when she wasn't checking on Sam, but she'd welcomed the activity. She'd even started an elaborate supper and was tending to the evening chores that Sam normally performed—anything to keep her thoughts occupied. Only now, while she waited for the water to fill the horse trough, she was forced to stop, to wait, to look into her deepest self and to acknowledge the truth that she'd kept at bay through sheer force of will until this moment.

*I could have lost him.* A tremor of fear and pain shook her, closed her throat with grief and despair. *And he'd never have known how much I love him.*

Roni placed her forehead on her arms and let the tears fall. The moment she'd seen Sam in the emergency room, bloody and battered, the truth smacked her in the face and opened her eyes. Yes, she'd adored Jessie from the minute she saw her and wanted to make a home for her, but the real reason Roni had married Sam Preston was that she was in love with him—madly, passionately, eternally—and probably had been for a very long time. Only, that certainly wasn't what Sam had bargained for. Talk about false pretenses.

No wonder she'd been jealous of the likes of Nadine Scott. Perhaps even her relationship with Jackson had been tainted because she'd judged every man she'd ever known by Sam's standard. But now, even though she found herself married to the man she adored, he only saw her as a good friend and a competent helpmate. And after last night's disaster, he probably would never desire her as a bed companion again. Feeling helpless and hopeless, she sobbed against her forearm.

"Jeez, Curly, don't do this." Sam's sleep-roughed voice was low in her ear, and his warm hands closed about her shoulders.

With a gasp, she whirled to face him, making her skirt swirl around her calves, scrubbing at the moisture trailing down her cheeks in embarrassment. "You—you shouldn't be up."

He tucked his hands into his front jeans pockets, inspecting her with a hooded expression. His clean chambray shirt hung open down the front, revealing a tanned slash of hair-dusted chest, and his cheekbone was swollen and bruised. "I'm okay."

"You need another pain pill? How about something to eat?" She was already moving past him, but he clamped a hand down on her shoulder, stopping her.

"No, I don't need anything—except to know why you're crying."

Alarmed, uncertain, she looked anywhere but at him. "It's nothing. I'm just silly... I've got to check dinner."

"I see." He dropped his hand. The slanted rays of the sun caught the highlights of his hair. "Well, you don't have to fret. I won't bother you again."

Her voice was a whisper of disbelief. "What?"

"It couldn't have been clearer how unpleasant last night was for you, Curly. And now..." He indicated her tear-streaked features with a brief wave. "Hell, I'm not going to force anything on you that you find that awful. And it kills me to see you cry. So you can quit worrying—"

She finally found her voice. "Is that what you think? You thick-headed puncher, how can you be so—so obtuse?"

"Well, what else?"

"You could have been killed today," she raged, fists clenching. Then she choked, and fresh tears spilled from her lashes. "I've never been so scared in all my life!"

"Oh, honey..." Sam's features twisted, and he reached for her. Then she was in his arms, clinging to his neck and weeping into his shirtfront.

"I couldn't bear to lose you, Sam," she sobbed.

"Hey, it's just a little scratch."

"You don't understand." Her voice was broken. "How can you not know?"

He threaded soothing fingers through the hair at her temple, tilting her face up to his. "Know what?"

"That I'm crazy in love with you."

Stunned, his eyes widened. "Holy Jehoshaphat."

"I can't help it, Sam. I'm sorry. I know you don't want it, didn't expect it, but there aren't any strings. I just want to be with you."

His voice was rough. "I'm not going anywhere."

"You don't have to feel obligated," she said in a rush. "Or say things you don't feel, but you did want me...at least up until last night."

"You think that's changed?" he growled.

"But you said—"

"Aw, hell, woman, you talk too much."

Jerking her close, Sam bent his head and proceeded to kiss her senseless. She responded with all the pent-up fervor produced by the past twenty-four hours' emotional roller-coaster ride, meeting his demands, opening her lips for his intimate exploration, pressing against him shamelessly.

His mouth was voracious, and his hands everywhere, palming her bottom, slipping inside the soft knit of her tank top to cup her breasts, unfettered by any bra today. Her core liquefied, sweet hot honey running though her veins like the final shafts of evening sunshine spearing through the air.

When he raised his head, they were both breathing hard, and Roni was so bemused that she hardly registered the cool dampness seeping through her sandals. Then she realized the water trough was overflowing, spreading a bog of mud in a circle around them.

"The water," she croaked.

Sam glanced down, reached over and twisted the spigot, then swept her up with one arm so fast, she gasped.

"Sam, your stitches . . . be careful."

"I'll holler when I'm hurt." He hitched a heel on the bottom rung of the corral and set her down on his knee. Sliding off her muddy sandals, he dangled her feet into the trough and began to splash her bare legs, rubbing his fingers up and down her calves, dampening the sheer gauze of her Gypsy skirt.

She shivered. "What are you doing?"

"Washing off your feet." His hand traveled above her knee, pushing back the fabric, then ran farther up her inner thigh.

"That's what I thought," she gasped. "I could get to like it, I think."

"Me, too." Bending her over his arm, he kissed her again, tantalizing her with little wet forays up her legs.

Quivering, Roni rubbed her fingers through the soft bramble of hair covering his hard-planed chest, found the bronze coins of his nipples and scored them lightly with her nails. He shuddered uncontrollably, and she smiled against his lips, sliding her hands toward his waistband.

"Not so fast." Lifting his head, he caught her wrist, gazing down into her breathless expression with a lambent heat in his eyes.

She was already past pretense. "I want you, Sam."

"Thank God."

Scooping her up in his arms, he carried her into the shadowy interior of the barn. Setting her to her feet against the rough board wall, he undid her braid and spread her hair across her shoulders, kissing her, exploring her throat with his lips, licking the salty taste of her from the hollow where her pulse jumped erratically.

Catching the strap of her tank top with one crooked finger, he drew it down her shoulder, then repeated the operation so that the garment puddled at her waist and her breasts were bared to his heated gaze. He brushed the backs of his knuckles against her nipples and watched them harden and pucker into rosy pebbled buds.

"Oh, sweet heaven, you're beautiful," he breathed, his tone reverent.

"You are, too." Her hands were urgent, pushing his shirt down his arms so that he was bare-chested, as well. "A beautiful man, scars and all."

Almost as if he couldn't help himself, he bent and brushed a kiss in the damp hollow between her breasts, then ran his lips over their upper swell. Roni groaned, needing him to touch her, and she took his jaw between her hands and guided him to the burgeoning tip, nearly fainting with pleasure as he took it into his mouth and suckled strongly.

"Oh, Sam!"

"Like that?" he murmured against her flesh.

"Uh-huh."

"Just tell me, sweetheart. Show me what you want."
Holding her by the waist, he let her guide him to a similar
performance on the other breast, licking and nipping and
teasing until she cried out in delight.

Overwhelmed, Roni let the sensations take her, melting
her bones, warming her blood. She loved the fine texture of
his hair against her fingers, and the unique scent of him—
leather and sandalwood and musk. She loved *him*. Rubbing her hands over his shoulders, she lightly traced the
outline of his bandage, regretting his hurt with all her being, yet grateful that he was still here with her, still hers and
loving her into jelly.

When she didn't think she could endure the exquisite
torture of his lips on her nipples another minute, he
dropped to one knee and bunched her skirts around her
hips, running his hands up the length of her thighs.

"Sam, what—oh!" She gasped in surprise and clutched
at his shoulders as he tasted her through the thin silk tri-
angle of her black bikini panties. "You can't—"

"Watch me." With a twist of his strong fingers, he
snapped the black satin ribbons holding the panties at her
hips, then cupped her buttocks to hold her immobile while
his tongue did wicked things to her.

Gasping, her head reeling, Roni's heart raced and her
excitement built, centering in the place where Sam was fast
driving her beyond coherence. She quivered, feeling herself losing all semblance of control, but he held her still,
allowing no resistance, delving with his tongue and fingertip into the dewy petals, feasting on her intimately until
sensation exploded and she cried out.

Standing, he caught her as she sagged against the barn
wall, capturing the final echo of that tremulous sound
within his own mouth as he kissed her deeply. Inhaling his

breath, she tasted her own essence and the sharpness of his arousal, and the fire that had barely subsided began to flame again.

Frantic, she fumbled at his belt buckle, loosing it and sliding her hands beneath his waistband, cupping and cradling the heavy weight of his engorged sex, reveling in the sight and touch of her man, a man on fire for her. Moaning, Sam crushed her to him, then helped release his fly. She rose on her toes as he pulled her hips up, meeting him eagerly, then arching her neck with the fine shock of pleasure as he eased into her wetness.

Twining her leg around his, Roni locked herself against him, letting him fill her, complete her, holding on for dear life as the universe quaked. Sam pressed his mouth against her neck and braced one hand against the wall at her back, moving in a rhythm that took her breath. Faster and faster, he made her his in a way she'd never dreamed, spinning her through a kaleidoscope of sensations until she catapulted over the edge of ecstasy again.

At her heartfelt cry, Sam loosed his own control, plunging into her with a powerful thrust, then shuddering at his own completion, holding her hips against him as though he could absorb her, making the two of them truly one being. Shaking, shuddering, they clung to each other, leaning weakly against the wall, their bodies still joined, slick with moisture and the sweet aftershocks of release.

Catching her face between his hands, Sam licked at her lips, nibbled at her chin. Satisfied beyond all imagining, she threaded her fingers into his hair and stretched like a cat, languid and sensual and murmuring.

"What was that?" he asked, his mouth against the pulse in her throat.

Her throaty chuckle made his body leap. "I said, that's more like it, cowboy."

He drew back to grin at her, his smoky blue eyes dancing wickedly with promise. "Lady, you ain't seen nothin' yet!"

# Eight

He was as good as his word.

"That's a disgustingly smug look on your face, Mrs. Preston."

"Uh-uh." Roni smiled at Sam's lazy comment, but didn't open her eyes. The morning sun streaming through the bedroom window fell across the tumbled sheets and their tangled, love-dampened bodies.

"A cat-lapping-cream expression, in fact."

She snuggled closer to him with a sigh of contentment. "Mmm."

Barely contained amusement made his voice gravelly. "I might even say, you've acquired a look-at-me-I've-been-thoroughly-ravished aspect."

Roni's smile grew wider, and she allowed her fingers to drift down the flat plane of Sam's belly. "I'll remind you that you have only yourself to blame, Mr. Preston."

Chest shaking with laughter, he caught her wrist. "You, ma'am, are shameless."

Laughing now, Roni swiftly straddled him, holding him down with her hands to his shoulders and grinning at him mischievously. "Aren't you glad?"

Sam's eyes darkened at the vision of naked wanton hovering above him. "Damn straight I am."

Hooking an arm around her neck, he pulled her down, kissing her deeply, thanking his lucky stars for this moment, for this woman. They'd loved throughout the night, making up for everything that had gone wrong that first time, exploring each other, moving into realms of passion and tenderness Sam had never thought to experience.

What a surprise she was! Alternately shy and bold, teasing and demure, but always willing, eager for him, meeting each advance of his with a sensual parry of her own. He couldn't get enough of her, reaching for her again and again, making up with a vengeance for all those weeks of frustration.

He marveled at how well they fit, how passion and familiarity and yet the uniqueness of their new intimacy melded into something extraordinary. The future lay before them like a golden river on which to sail. If he felt a pang that he could not return her profession of love, that was quickly squelched by the knowledge of what he could give her in terms of physical affection. And with male pride, Sam knew he'd satisfied her over and over. It would be more than enough.

Yes, they were a matched set now, paired for life, and he was determined to enjoy every minute of it. Lifting her hips, he guided her onto himself, groaning in pleasure at the way she gloved him, warm and tight, and prepared to do just that.

* * *

"You keep this up and neither of us will be able to walk," Roni gasped in mock protest sometime later.

"I'm willing to risk it."

She gave a rueful chuckle. "Easy for you to say."

"Oh, yeah? You've just about crippled me." Rising from the bed, Sam hobbled to the door, evoking more giggles from Roni. "Not that I'm complaining, mind you."

The white bandage across his shoulder blade was a stark contrast to his bronzed back, and she frowned slightly at the sight of it. "All this, uh, activity didn't hurt your back, did it?"

"Believe me, I had other things on my mind." He waggled his eyebrows Groucho-style. "Want to share a shower, Curly?"

Rolling her eyes, she pitched a pillow at him and snuggled down in the sheets. "Are you always this insatiable?"

"Only where you're concerned."

That pleased her enormously, and she gave him a smile that took his breath.

"You're very tempting. . . ." The bedside phone jangled, and she reached for it with a disappointed sigh. "That's probably Krystal wondering what's going on."

"A humdinger of a honeymoon, that's what. Think she would keep Jessie another night?"

Hand on the receiver, Roni laughed and shook her head. "Go take that shower. Better make it a cold one!"

Sam came back to the bed, kissed her senseless and murmured against her lips, "Won't do a bit of good, Curly. I've got it bad for you, and that's a fact."

He walked to the bathroom, leaving Roni stunned and melting. Making love with Sam was the most glorious thing she'd ever experienced, and joy filled every cell of her being. So what if he hadn't said he loved her? Every tenderness, every caress, every kiss said it louder than any words ever could. He was gun-shy, too hurt by his first wife's desertion to risk that kind of commitment yet, but it didn't matter. They had time to spare, time to grow together and learn the depths of each other's souls, and Roni had no doubt that one day Sam would say the words she longed to hear. She hugged the certainty to herself.

The phone rattled under her hand again, and she came out of her bemused state with a start of surprise. "Uh, hello? Oh, hi, Mom."

"Are you all right, Veronica?" Carolyn asked, her voice tinny on the line. "You sound odd."

Blushing, Roni plumped pillows against the headboard and sat up, pulling the sheet over her breasts. "Everything's fine, Mom."

"Sam and the baby?"

"Just wonderful. When are you coming to see how much Jessie's grown?"

"Actually, Jinks wants to drive in for the Flat Fork rodeo on Saturday. We'll spend the night at the old house, if that's okay."

Roni curled a lock of hair around her forefinger, listening to the sound of Sam's deep voice as he sang off-key in the shower. A shower with new pipes and nozzle and knobs, and every cent of the check she'd written to Steve Cutler was worth it for the enjoyment Sam was getting. She felt a twinge of regret that she hadn't joined him, then perked up. There was always next time.

"Roni, are you there?" her mother asked. "You know, the rodeo—parade, barbecue, events?"

Roni focused her wandering attention. "Oh, is that this weekend?"

"You mean you forgot the biggest shindig of the year in that little town? Honestly, where is your mind these days?"

"I've been kind of busy, Mom."

Carolyn's voice went dry. "I can imagine. That Sam is one good-looking cowpuncher."

"Mom!"

"Now don't go all prudish on me, Veronica Jean. You're not the daughter I raised if you aren't making the most of a man who obviously adores you. Are you happy, honey?"

A soft smile curled Roni's mouth. "Yes, Mama, I am. Deliriously happy."

"Good. That's what I told Jackson."

"What?"

"That no-good scoundrel called here looking for you."

Roni frowned and sat up straighter. "He did? What did he want?"

"Something about a job you did for him on *Apache Tears* being so impressive, his producers want you for another project."

Roni gave an indelicate snort. "That's about Jackson's speed all right. Still trying to get something for nothing."

"I don't know," Carolyn mused. "He did say the word *hire* at least once, and he sounded pretty desperate."

"Well, at least that's a switch. But I'm not interested in helping Jackson out of his latest frying pan, and he hasn't called."

"No, I wouldn't give him Sam's number until I'd checked it with you first."

"Thanks, Mom. Having Jackson call here is the last thing I need."

"I did say I'd pass on his number if you were interested."

"Well, I'm not. But if he should happen to call back, tell him I can be hired—at an exorbitant fee—and to take it up with my agent. Knowing Jackson, that should end the matter."

"I always knew you were a sensible girl." There was a gabble of talk on the other end, then Carolyn said, "Jinks says hello, and we'll see you on Saturday."

"We'll look forward to it." Hanging up the phone, Roni chewed her lip and stared off into space, more than a little befuddled by this unexpected intrusion back into her life by Jackson Dial.

"Problem?" Sam stood in the doorway, a towel draped around his hips, scrubbing his fingers through his damp hair.

"Huh?" Coming to, Roni made an instant decision. Things with Sam were so new and so good, she didn't want to risk even a moment of disharmony with something as immaterial and passé as her old flame. She shook her head. "No problem. Just my mother telling me about someone trying to track me down for a job, but I'm not interested. By the way, she and Jinks are coming for the rodeo this weekend."

"It'll be great to see them."

Roni tilted her head and gave Sam an innocent look. "Say, can I ride Diablo in the parade?"

"What? Are you out of your ever-loving mind?" He cast a jaundiced eye over her sultry smile and the forefinger she crooked at him in invitation. "Oh no, you don't, Curly..."

"What's the matter, cowboy?" she pouted. "Afraid of a little old-fashioned horse trading?"

"In a word, yes. Woman, I think you're dangerous." His blue eyes glinted as he dropped his towel. "But then I've always been a man who liked living on the edge."

With a rousing rendition of "The Yellow Rose of Texas," the Flat Fork High School Mustang Marching Band led the annual rodeo parade past the boisterous crowds lining the sidewalks of downtown Flat Fork. Colorful floats sponsored by the local 4-H Clubs, Lions Club, Boy Scouts and various churches and businesses followed the band on this hot and sunny Saturday afternoon, and nearly one hundred mounted cowboys and cowgirls decked out in every sort of raiment from silver-trimmed Spanish saddles to Indian war paint and sequins to a simple working cowboy's leather tack brought up the rear.

Seated proudly near the front of the pack atop a prancing Diablo, Roni couldn't contain a grin of pure delight. Other women might have diamond rings and dozens of red roses as proof of their lover's devotion, but she had Sam's precious ebony stallion—at least for the moment—and his indulgence of her whim gave her a warm fuzzy feeling that made her heart bubble over in happiness.

As they approached the courthouse square, Roni searched the crowd eagerly, then spotted the tall blond man in a bright blue Western shirt and white hat identical to her own. He held a bright-eyed baby cowgirl with flyaway russet curls whose miniature shirt matched her parents'—an indulgence in family pride that was almost expected in the warm extended community of Flat Fork. Carolyn and Bud stood beside Sam and Jessie, watching over a stroller with a trio of helium balloons tied to it.

"Jessie . . . hi, baby!" Roni waved. Sam pointed her out to the child. The little girl frowned, waved uncertainly, then suddenly dimpled and blew her mother a kiss. Roni laughed and returned the gesture.

"Love you, too, sweetie." She shouted over the tumult to Sam, hoping he could read her lips. "Meet you at the fairgrounds."

Sam nodded his acknowledgment and gave her a thumbs-up.

As the parade moved toward the outskirts of town where the rodeo arena was located, Roni chatted with the other riders and enjoyed the camaraderie among her old friends and neighbors. The field used as a parking lot was a jumble of vehicles and horse trailers, and the pungent odors of the fairgrounds—hay, cotton candy, chili peppers, manure and diesel exhaust from the carnival rides—greeted her as they approached.

Roni was looking forward to having a little fun with her husband today—watching Jessie take her first ride on a merry-go-round, eating barbecue until they popped, cheering on the local rodeo cowboys as they tried their luck against bulls and broncos and the clock. While she'd certainly had no complaints about Sam's attentions, he and his crew had worked like the devil all week carting livestock back and forth for Buzz Henry's perusal. And it had been an impressive presentation. Sam was cautiously optimistic about the chance of landing the contract, but the pressure was immense with so much at stake. It wouldn't hurt the man to take some time off with his family and enjoy himself.

As the parade broke up at the fairground's gate, everything became a mass of confusion with floats and riders going in a hundred different directions at once, trucks being cranked, shouts of recognition and greeting as groups of families and friends reunited. Roni clucked softly at Diablo and tapped him with her heels, guiding him through the melee toward Sam's truck and the horse trailer they'd parked earlier. The others were driving Roni's Jeep for convenience.

But Diablo, who'd been the perfect gentleman all through the parade itself, suddenly wasn't sure that he liked all the furor going on around them. He danced sideways, his ears pricked, while Roni struggled to control him.

"Whoa, Diablo. Cut it out, darn you!"

A souped-up truck blasted past, country music blaring out of the teenager's megawatt sound system. Startled, Diablo pivoted, ignoring Roni's commands, and for a dismayed moment she was sure she was headed for an ignominious "tail over teakettle" landing. But then a rider on a dappled gray Appaloosa caught Diablo's bridle, and the big stallion instantly quieted down again.

"Hey, you all right?"

"Fine, thanks. Much obliged." Grappling with the reins and her racing heart, Roni looked up to find Travis King watching her with a wicked twinkle in his dark eyes. "Travis! My gosh, how are you?"

He pulled the brim of his black hat in an automatic cowboy courtesy, and a grin lifted his mustache. "Roni. Could be better, but can't complain, I guess. Mighty fine piece of hoss you got there. Which way you headed?"

"Just over there." Roni indicated the horse trailer emblazoned with the Lazy Diamond brand. Releasing Diablo's bridle, Travis kicked his mount into place beside Roni and they headed side by side toward the trailer.

"I can't thank you enough, Travis," Roni said. "If I'd eaten dust, Sam would never have let me live it down."

"Powerful animal for a little lady like you."

Roni grimaced as they dismounted at the trailer. "That's what Sam said. I guess he's right, but don't tell him I said so."

"Ole Sam . . . he sure likes being right, doesn't he?"

There was an awkward space as their eyes met and they acknowledged the burdens of the past. Roni shrugged, both helpless and regretful. "Well, you know Sam."

"You're good for him, I'll bet. He's a lucky man."

"And you're still the sweet-talkin'-est bull rider I ever saw." Her smile was warm. "What are you doing here, anyway?"

"A little of this and that. You know, business, personal appearance, make the hometown crowd happy."

Travis pulled his mecate reins through his gloved hand, and Roni noticed his movements were stiff. She remembered what Krystal had said about his rodeo injuries and wondered just how serious they were. Battered or not, though, Travis King was still a fine-looking specimen of a man, and Roni was sure that he had a passel of "buckle bunnies" waiting on the sidelines for him in every rodeo town.

"Well, Flat Fork loves to hail the conquering hero," she said. "Ought to be fun for you."

He chuckled, but there was an ironic twist to his lips. "Some hero. Look, I put a business proposition to Sam a while back. Tell him it's still open if he changes his mind."

Roni bit her lip and nodded. "I will, but..."

"Yeah, I know. He's a stubborn cuss." Travis indicated Diablo. "You need any help with his tack?"

"I can handle it, thanks. And Sam will be here soon."

"I'll get moving, then. You take care of yourself." He pulled his hat brim again.

"You, too, Travis."

She watched him remount, noting again a certain hesitation in his movements that did not bode well for his continued career as a top bull rider. Something told her that is was time for Travis King to hang up his spurs. Turning to unsaddle Diablo, Roni shook her head. What was it about stubborn men, anyway? Sometimes it seemed they never learned.

The rest of Roni's party caught up with her just as she finished wiping Diablo down. They left the horse tethered with a full feed bag and then adjourned to the Jaycee barbecue stand for an early supper.

Later, before the rodeo, Roni and Carolyn pushed Jessie around the midway in her stroller while Jinks and Sam strolled behind, occasionally trying their hands at the carnival games in an attempt to see who could win the biggest teddy bear for Jessie. When the men decided to throw baseballs at milk bottles and Jessie was happily going around and around on a tiny tots airplane ride, Carolyn gave her daughter another news report.

"Jackson called again this week."

"Did you give him my message?" Roni asked, waving at Jessie as she made another loop.

"Yes, but he didn't sound too happy."

"Do you know what's nice about all this, Mom?" Roni grinned. "I couldn't care less about Mr. Dial's problems."

"Anyone with eyes can see that married life agrees with you."

"It's Sam who agrees with me. He's perfect. We're perfect."

Carolyn's answering smile flickered. "That's as it should be, honey. But you'd best remember Sam's just a man like any other. Marriage is hard enough work as it is. Don't go building up expectations of perfection. You're bound to be disappointed."

"And you're bound to be a worry wart. I guess that comes with being a mother. I'm finding that out. But don't worry, everything with Sam and me is fine, just fine."

Reassured, Carolyn hugged her daughter. "Of course. Look, there's Krystal. Haven't those boys of hers grown?"

Krystal and Bud and their three towheaded sons joined the group, and after a few more rides, they all made their way into the arena and found seats on the board bleachers just as the sun disappeared behind the horizon and the first evening star appeared in the darkening sky.

"Having fun?" Sam murmured in Roni's ear.

"Yep." She settled Jessie in her lap and innocently placed her hand on Sam's knee.

Covering her fingers, he rubbed them suggestively up and down his denim-covered thigh. "But not as much fun as we'll have later, right?"

She cast him a provocative look under her lashes. "We'll have to see how the night progresses."

"Promises, promises."

"Only for you, cowboy."

They stood as the announcer introduced the mounted color guard and the playing of the national anthem. Afterward, they cheered and gasped as the rapid-fire events unfolded—calf roping and steer wrestling, barrel racing and bronco busting. Midway through, the announcer's voice boomed over the speakers, demanding that everyone give a Flat Fork howdy to one of their own, two-time champion bull rider Travis King.

Roni noticed instantly how Sam stiffened and his eyes narrowed as Travis stepped out from near the chutes to wave his hat at the crowd and take a bow. Roni wondered for a moment if Travis intended to compete in the upcoming bull riding events, then was relieved when he merely headed for the media box at the top of the bleachers. But she didn't like the hard look in Sam's eye as he watched his competitor for Buzz Henry's contract mount the stairs.

"Travis is moving kind of slow these days, isn't he?" she asked.

"One too many rank bulls, I guess."

"He was nice enough to give me a hand with Diablo earlier." Bouncing Jessie, who was becoming more fractious by the minute, Roni turned to warn off Krystal's youngest. "No, honey, she's had enough cotton candy. It'll make her sick."

"Here, let me." Sam lifted the tired and sticky baby and settled her against his broad shoulder. The other members of the group were engrossed in the bull riding.

Relieved of Jessie's weight, Roni sighed. Leaning on her elbows onto the seat behind her, she fixed her husband with a questioning look and spoke in a low tone. "Why don't you consider his offer, Sam? He said to tell you it's still open."

His jaw grew taut. "You know why."

"Yes, but when are you going to let it go?"

"We've been over this ground, Curly."

"Okay, okay. But to cut off your nose to spite your face is pretty damned childish, don't you think? Especially considering circumstances at the Lazy Diamond."

"You let me worry about that. It's not your concern, all right?"

"No, it's not all right!" She sat up straight, frowning. "We're partners, aren't we?"

He rubbed Jessie's back, chuckling. "After the last few days, I'd say more than that."

Flushing, Roni responded with an angry hiss. "I don't mean just in bed! I'm a part of this family, too. You've got to let me in if this is going to work."

"Honey, as far as I'm concerned, it's working just fine."

"But—"

Bending his head, he silenced her with a swift kiss, a shocking thing for a private man like Sam Preston to do in such a public place.

"Now, now, you two." Krystal's teasing voice broke them apart. "There are children present. Set an example."

"Yeah, Sam," Bud joked. "Show me that move again. Like this?"

Bud bussed Krystal soundly, breaking up the group with laughter and receiving a playful slap from his giggling wife for his efforts.

After that, the talk turned general again, so Roni had no option but to let Sam's remarks pass. They niggled at her, however, filling her with a nebulous uneasiness. As close as she and Sam had become, she knew that he held something of himself back at all times, as if he didn't trust her to be completely on his side, and the knowledge hurt. And although she did trust Sam, and knew she could always depend on him, in a chilling sort of way his withholding of himself was more in the mold of Jackson Dial than she cared to consider.

Jessie fussed against Sam's shoulder, drawing Roni's attention. "It's way past her bedtime. I'd better take her home."

After bidding everyone good-night, Sam walked his ladies across the pasture parking lot to Roni's Jeep. The plaintive melody of the carousel carried over the muted roar of the people still enjoying the midway.

"I'll bring Diablo's trailer when I come," Sam said. "Don't worry if I'm late. I'm going to try to get another word in with Buzz after things finish up here tonight."

Roni buckled Jessie into her car seat. The little girl murmured drowsily and fell instantly asleep. "Do you think he might be ready to make a decision?"

"I hope he already has—in favor of the Lazy Diamond. But I'm not about to let Travis King get a jump on me if he hasn't."

"Oh, Sam." With a disappointed sigh she slid into the driver's seat.

"Look, I'm not in the mood for another lecture, okay?"

There was a tension and a sharpness in Sam's voice that surprised and wounded her. But they'd all had a long day, and she knew that now wasn't the time for her to push a resolution of the uncertainties that still remained in their relationship, much less his unresolved feelings toward Travis King.

"Whatever you want, Sam," she murmured, starting the engine.

He leaned in through the window, his features softening. "I want *you*, Curly, but duty calls." He dropped a quick peck on her lips. "Keep your fingers crossed, and maybe when I get home tonight we'll really have something to celebrate."

*If it weren't for bad luck, I'd have no luck at all....*

With an angry flick of his wrist, Sam turned off the truck radio, killing the country singer's mournful crooning. He filled up the empty space with a string of curses that didn't let up until he parked the truck and horse trailer beside the barn back at the Lazy Diamond. Climbing out, he cast a quick look toward the ranch house. A single light shone, but he could hardly bear to look at it. God, what was he going to tell Roni?

Slamming the truck door, Sam gave the rear tire a savage kick of pure frustration. Buzz Henry's hope-destroying words still rang in his ears.

*Sorry, Sam, but I got to go with King's outfit this year. Maybe next season...*

By next season it could be too late. Sam unchained the rear of the horse trailer and walked Diablo free. His hands lingered on the animal, soothing and praising without words, and the stallion wickered softly, butting his forehead against Sam's shoulder. Sam felt like a traitor.

"Sorry, ole buddy. Old Man Henderson's been after me to buy you for years. Looks like I don't have much choice now."

With a slap on the rump, Sam turned the horse into his corral and latched the gate, a simple enough chore, but the normalcy of his actions was totally at odds with the blasted, barren terrain inside his soul. Adversity was supposed to make a man stronger, wasn't it? Well, Sam was just tired. Tired of struggling, tired of fighting, but what the hell else was he supposed to do? The Lazy Diamond was his life.

But it wasn't just him anymore. No, Roni and Jessie were his responsibilities, and Roni sure as hell hadn't signed on just to find out the ship was sinking. A cold, clenching fear settled in his gut when he thought of her reaction. Well, his back was truly against the wall, and he'd have to retrench if he hoped to salvage anything out of this mess. The problem was, at the moment he didn't have an inkling what to do next.

But that was nothing new, either. For years, he'd been hiding his fears and his worries, drawing from some unknown source of strength within himself to keep going. His mouth twisted. Sam Preston, strong and silent and stalwart. What a damned joke. But there was nothing for him to do now but play out the hand. Drawing a steadying breath, Sam squared his shoulders and went to the house.

He found Roni at the kitchen table engrossed in some kind of letter. She wore one of those damnable silky kimono robe things, and, from the way his heart lurched, probably nothing under it. Her dark hair was loose, falling down her back the way he liked, and her bare feet curled over the rungs of the kitchen chair. At his entrance, she looked up with an abstracted smile.

"Hi. I waited—" Her expression snapped into focus, and she sat up, alarmed. "What is it? What's wrong?"

Sam grimaced. So much for keeping up a stone face to spare her the bad news. She'd read him like a book. Jaw clenched, he hooked his hat on a peg and turned to her with the bald truth.

"I didn't get the contract. Buzz told me he's giving it to Travis King."

She blinked, but no words of commiseration or sympathy fell from her lips. Instead, she glanced down at the paper in her hands and said slowly, "That settles it, then. I'm going to Hollywood."

# Nine

___

"**J**ust like that?"

Sam looked as though she'd punched him in the gut. With a start, Roni realized what she'd said.

"No, Sam, of course not." She jumped to her feet, waving the letter. "Let me explain."

"What's to explain?" The bitterness in his voice chilled her to the bone. "The belt around here gets tightened another notch, and you turn tail and run. Just like Shelly."

She flushed angrily, but kept her gaze steady. "That was uncalled for."

"Yeah, well, if the boot fits..."

"Shut up!" She controlled herself with an effort, then spoke between gritted teeth, slowly, as if to a stubborn and none-too-bright child. "I've had a job offer. A very lucrative offer. One that will make it possible to keep the Lazy Diamond running. But I'll have to go to California. So now you just leap back over those conclusions you've been jumping to, mister!''

"What job?" he growled suspiciously. "For whom? Doing what?"

"Preliminary art design for a new movie. It's a fabulous opportunity for me professionally. The backers were especially insistent that I come aboard, which is very flattering, and the fee my agent has arranged—" Referring to the letter, she named a figure that still amazed her, a sum that could mean all the difference to the Lazy Diamond. "So you see, it's a godsend. A proverbial gift horse."

"What's this horse's name?"

She swallowed, for this was the difficult part. "Uh, it's Jackson, Sam."

"Jackson Dial? As in your former *significant other?* And I'm supposed to go for this idea?" He threw his hands up. "You're crazy. And so is he. Forget it. No way. End of discussion."

"You're being totally unreasonable."

"If you think I'll let my *wife* run back to her old lover—"

"Jackson doesn't mean a thing to me anymore, and you know it!" she shouted, infuriated. She shook the letter at him. "Look, this is a way out for us, that's all."

Sam snatched the paper and ripped it in half, letting the pieces fall to the kitchen tiles. "By God, I can take care of my own without Jackson Dial's charity."

"It is not charity," she replied indignantly. "I'm good at what I do, and I earn my fee and then some. And for your information, Jackson isn't exactly thrilled at the situation, either, but *Apache Tears* is winning all kinds of artistic awards and his financiers are insisting I do the work again."

"How very convenient," he said with a sneer.

"He's begging me, Sam, and he's so desperate, he's willing to come up to scratch with the money for the first time." She lifted her chin defiantly. "After all the years I wasted on him, having the shoe on the other foot is very sweet."

"I'll bet. And now that he finally sees what a gem you are, he'll make good in other areas, I suppose? Too bad you're a married woman."

Crossing her arms, she glared at him and her voice was deadly quiet. "You say something that asinine again, and I'm going to throw something at you, I swear."

"Be my guest." He waved a hand expansively. "Just don't think I'm swallowing any of this garbage about careers and helping out an old flame meaning nothing. There's only one reason you'd even consider this, and that's because you want to. I guess Flat Fork can't compete with L.A.'s bright lights."

"Oh, you stubborn...*cowboy*. Here's the perfect opportunity to get the Lazy Diamond solvent again. What's wrong with that?"

"I told you, I can take care of my own."

"Oh, is that what you call this?" Anger sharpened her voice with sarcasm. "Too damn stubborn to throw in with Travis when you could, so now no contract! And too prideful to sell off some land or reduce the stock, because that might show the world you've failed. Well, Sam, you've got a busted truck, no credit and a wife and daughter to support. How's your pride going to feel when the bank forecloses on the Lazy Diamond?"

"That's enough."

"It hurts to hear the truth, doesn't it?"

"I said that's enough, Curly."

Her lower lip trembled. "Well, it hurts me, too, Sam. It hurts when you won't treat me as an equal partner. I can help. I *want* to help. Don't you know the Lazy Diamond is important to me, too? My earnings would take the pressure off, allow us to regroup."

"Not this way. And anyway, I can't believe you'd consider leaving Jessie like that."

"I could take her with me...."

"Hell, no!"

"I agree it would be unwise to uproot her again. And I'll miss her like everything, but it'll only be for a few weeks. Can't you see, Sam? It's a chance I need to take. Let me do this for *us*."

His jaw was hard as iron. "I won't have it."

She looked at him a long moment, blinking back tears. "Do you think you really have a choice?"

"Don't push me, Curly."

"Sam, please—"

He yanked his hat from the peg and stomped to the door. "I mean it, woman. I'll figure something out, don't you worry, and it won't mean taking advantage of your all-mighty beneficence or selling out to the likes of Jackson Dial, either. You cross me on this, and you'll regret it."

The door slammed behind him. Roni gulped and pressed trembling fingers to her mouth to contain the sobs that threatened to break something free inside her chest. Stunned by the violence of Sam's rejection of her and her offer, she stood immobile while hot tears streaked down her face.

What was the matter with him? Couldn't he see she was just trying to help? Or did his rejection lie in something deeper, something she'd chosen to ignore in her recent euphoric state?

Doubts assailed her. She'd pushed for the marriage, pushed until he'd had to take her into his bed or deny his very manhood, pushed for him to let her into his heart and *really* into his life. She realized now it was all arrogance on her part, her cock certainty that Sam would come to love her, that he needed her as much as she needed him.

But it was abundantly clear now that there were territories he would never allow her to enter, places inside of him that he held sacrosanct and inviolate. And in the spot where Roni hid all of her secret fears and insecurities, she knew it was because he didn't love her. Desired her, yes. Respected and admired her, perhaps. But willing to drop all of his defenses and let her see him as he truly was, out of naked honesty and love, no.

And the most devastating realization was that there was nothing she could do to make it happen.

A part of her soul shriveled. What was wrong with her that she was unable to evoke the kind of devotion she yearned for from the men she cared about? Was it a genetic tendency? Something in her makeup that made her choose the wrong man again and again? A deficiency in her own feminine nature that attracted the terminally commitment phobic?

Anguished, Roni stumbled to their bedroom and threw herself down on the coverlet. *We're friends,* she told herself as she wept into Sam's pillow. But why hadn't she foreseen that it wouldn't be enough? And that thought kept haunting her....

She came awake at the creak of the bed frame and the feel of his hands on her. "Oh, Sam, I didn't—"

His mouth covered hers, staking a powerful claim as he silenced her. After that, he never let her have breath enough to speak, nor did he say anything himself. Kissing her relentlessly, he stole her thoughts with his caresses, then pulled her beneath him and rode her to a completion so devastating that she cried out again and again as she clung to him.

He held her close as she sank into the exhausted haze of utter satisfaction, but her last conscious thought was a question. Was their cataclysmic joining an act of desperation on his part or hers?

It was a damned neat trick walking on eggshells in your Western boots, but Sam was fast becoming adept at it. He managed another half smile for something Carolyn was saying and wondered how much longer he could stand the pleasantries of this Sunday lunch with his in-laws.

Rosie's Café was filled with the after-church crowd, families in their Sunday best spilling out of the booths and tables around the minuscule dance floor. He was sure there'd been quite a party until the wee hours following the rodeo, a lot of two-stepping and cowboy romancing and maybe even a fist fight or two, but in the bright light spilling from the front windows the pine-paneled interior looked downright respectable, not counting the neon signs over the long, brass-railed bar advertising various brands of beer.

But Rosie's home-style cuisine was reason enough to draw a crowd at any time. The only sour note was the subtle tension at the corners of his wife's lovely mouth as she coaxed Jessie into another bite of rice and gravy.

"Watch she doesn't choke," Carolyn warned.

"Oh, Mom, she loves it. Look." Roni offered another spoonful of well-mashed beef tips and savory rice and Jessie lapped it up like a pro, beating her chubby fists against the tray of her high chair in approval.

Jinks leaned back from his saucer of lemon meringue pie and looked around for their waitress. "Think we could get some more coffee over here? You want another cup, Sam?"

"No, I'm fine." *Just wound tighter than a two-dollar watch.*

He didn't want to appear inhospitable, but he hoped Jinks and Carolyn wouldn't linger since they had the drive back to Austin ahead of them. Sam didn't know how much longer he could be sociable, not with Roni avoiding his eyes and barely sending two words his way since they'd dressed for church and headed to town.

Dammit, hadn't they worked out everything last night? Surely she'd put aside that bone-headed notion about working for Jackson Dial. And from the way she'd responded to his loving, she'd certainly forgiven him for flying off the handle at her. She was *his,* and he had proved it to her over and over, binding her to him in the best way he knew. Then why was she still so sulled up?

*Women.* Sam blew out a silent breath and looked across the dance floor to the booth where he and Roni had talked away so many Friday nights.

Things had been a whole lot simpler then when they were just friends. Not that he'd ever regret their becoming lovers, but it sure as hell complicated matters, at least in a woman's mind, giving her ideas and expectations despite anything a man did or didn't say. Maybe that was what was wrong with Roni this morning—her expectations had run head-on into the reality of their life together last night.

Well, a man had to hold on to certain standards or he wasn't much of a man. She'd touched a raw nerve with her talk about losing the Lazy Diamond, but she was wrong to underestimate his determination. There had to be another way to salvage his self-respect, and by God, he was going to find it.

He chanced a swift glance at Roni's averted profile. In her crisp cotton dress with its navy dots and a wide white collar, she was the image of the happy young matron at ease with her family. Only he knew that it was an act. Well, she'd get over her anger soon enough when she saw he wasn't budging on this issue.

Yeah, Roni was smart. She'd adjust. All he had to do was give it a little time.

*He needs more time,* Roni thought.

Time to cool off. Time to lower those masculine defenses, so that he could think clearly about the situation. Only, there wasn't a lot of that precious commodity that Roni could give him. Her agent's letter had made it clear Jackson had to have a decision pronto.

If only Sam would be reasonable. Well, she'd give him the rest of the day to stew, she decided, then approach him again tomorrow. Maybe by then his male ego would have deflated enough for him to see the logical benefits of this opportunity. If not . . .

Roni took a baby wipe from the diaper bag and mopped Jessie's gravy-stained mouth and fingers, playing a peek-a-boo game to keep her from fussing. Lord, she loved this baby! Why couldn't Sam understand that sometimes sacrifices were necessary for the good of a family?

*Family.* The word stopped her, made her shiver slightly. Was that what they were? Or had it all been a pretty pipe dream? Fear ballooned in her chest, a frightened idea that she'd totally misconstrued everything. Had finding herself in love with Sam blinded her? Maybe she hadn't realized the connection and intimacy and true partnership she'd believed that Sam was withholding out of his own fear was something that he simply wasn't capable of giving—now or ever—because his emotions had never been truly engaged.

Perhaps Sam still saw this all as a business proposition and, at the moment, one of the junior partners was bucking the will of the corporate boss. It was unclear to Roni whether the powerful way Sam had loved her during the night was an apology or merely an attempt to control her.

She shivered again. She didn't really want to know the answer to that.

"Veronica, are you all right?" Carolyn asked quietly.

"Huh?" Conscious that Sam's gaze was upon her, Roni knew he was waiting to see if she'd try to enlist Carolyn's support.

But that wasn't Roni's way. She wouldn't burden her mother with her problems, nor share confidences about the situation until they'd reached some resolution. And that could take some time. Roni forced a smile.

"Sure, Mom, I'm fine. Maybe a little tired. It's been a long weekend."

"For all of us. Jinks, honey, forget about that coffee. We need to get back on the road."

After Jinks and Sam wrangled good-naturedly over paying the tab, they all went outside to bid their adieus in the gravel parking lot.

"Wave bye-bye to Grandma, Jessie," Roni instructed.

The little girl dutifully waved as Jinks and Carolyn drove off, then demanded Sam's attention with a rapid "Da, da, da, da!"

Sam's expression had been rather stern throughout lunch, but now it thawed under Jessie's sunshiny smile.

Laughing softly, Roni passed him the baby. "You little toot! When are you going to say ma-ma?"

"In her own sweet time, like all women," Sam commented.

"Yes, I suppose." For a brief instant, the constraint had left her, but now it returned, leaving Roni feeling stiff and awkward as she reached to open the door of Sam's truck.

"Curly."

She looked up to find his blue eyes on her. "Yes, Sam?"

But he had no idea what it was he'd intended to say. "Uh, nothing. Let's get going. I've got a lot to do."

*Time,* he thought, driving the truck down the long road home.

*Time,* she thought, watching his hands on the steering wheel.

*Just give it a little time.*

It was time to take the bull by the horns.

"I need to give Jackson an answer."

Roni set a plate of sandwiches in front of her husband. He and the crew had taken a late lunch after a Monday morning of cutting hay, not a cowpuncher's favorite pastime by any means, but a necessary one, nonetheless. Sam's hair was wet from the dousing he'd given it washing up, and his cheekbones were rosy under his tan from the sun's harsh bite and his rapidly growing annoyance.

"Don't start this again." He picked up a turkey-lettuce-and-tomato-sandwich and took a bite, mumbling, "He's got his answer—forget it."

"No, Sam. That's *your* answer."

The sandwich hit the plate. "Dammit, Roni—"

"Lower your voice. You'll wake the baby."

"We're not going to discuss this again." He glared at her. "And I hate turkey."

"It's good for your cholesterol level, cowboy. And we *are* going to discuss my helping us out of our present bind in a cool and logical manner."

"Discuss all you want. It won't change anything."

"No?" Leaning against the sink, she crossed her arms over her paint-smeared T-shirt and pinned him with her gaze. "Have you found an alternative?"

"I'm working on it." He looked away. "I may have a buyer for Diablo."

She blinked, stricken. "Oh, Sam, no. Not Diablo."

He pushed the plate away. "He'll bring top dollar. Henderson's wanted him for a long time."

"But you meant to breed him yourself to improve your own stock."

"Yeah, well, plans can change."

"This is ridiculous." Picking up a dish towel, she began to wipe furiously at the already spotless counter. "There's no need for you to sacrifice Diablo. And his selling price would be a drop in the bucket anyway."

"I told you to let me worry about it."

"Well, it's not that easy. Other men's wives work. This whole country is filled with two-income families." She gave him a crooked smile and attempted to inject a little humor into the situation. "Anyway, don't they say that behind every successful rancher is a wife who works in town?"

"In town. Not across the country. And not for Jackson Dial."

"It's just another commission," she snapped, exasperated. Throwing down the towel, she snatched her latest sketch of Jessie's animals—coyotes and prairie dogs—off the refrigerator door and held it out. "Are you going to tell me not to try to sell this storybook? Or not to accept the next magazine cover?"

"That's not the same thing."

"It's exactly the same thing. What are you so afraid of? Do you think accepting my earnings will contaminate the Lazy Diamond or something?"

Balling up his paper napkin, he tossed it on his plate and rose with a scraping of chair legs. "This is useless."

"No, that's it, isn't it?" Her eyes widened. "If you accept my help, you have to acknowledge that I have a share in this ranch and this family, too. It might obligate you to open up a little, actually reveal something about your hopes and dreams, but you're just too yellow to risk it."

"I don't know what you're talking about."

"I'm talking about the fact that you're not so much jealous of my seeing Jackson again as interested in protecting your territory and your emotions." Her lips trembled suddenly. "Even against me."

"Jeez, don't you start crying. I can't stand it when you cry."

"Shelly slashed your heart and nearly took the Lazy Diamond, but you have to remember one thing—*I'm not Shelly.*"

"I know you're not."

"No, you merely treat me that way by your every deed and action. You hold me at arm's length, afraid to let me get too close on any level."

"Now you're the one being ridiculous and melodramatic."

She looked at him sadly, despairingly. "You don't get it, do you? You don't trust me. You live with me and share my bed, but you're afraid someday I'll put a knife in your back."

"I've got work to do."

"Sam—"

He grabbed his hat off the peg, then scooped up the remains of the sandwich. "I'll be back by suppertime."

The porch door slammed behind him, and Roni heard him gun the truck down the drive. She sat down at the table, realizing that she'd crushed the sketch in her fist. Deliberately, she smoothed it out with her palm, but the pastel colors smeared, spoiling hours of labor.

She'd gotten to the crux of the problem, she thought. How could she convince Sam to trust her? And that pride of his. Like a spirited stallion, she didn't want to break Sam so much as gentle him, but he couldn't see it.

*Patience,* she counseled herself. She sighed. And that meant refusing Jackson's offer, no matter what the cost to the Lazy Diamond, to her career or to her marriage. Stubborn, stubborn man!

Lips twisted in a grimace of resignation, Roni reached for the stack of letters Sam had brought in from the mailbox earlier and automatically sorted through them, her mind whirling, searching for alternatives and possibilities. She frowned curiously over an envelope from Cutler's Plumbing, slit it open, then stared in disbelief at the contents.

A note from Steve Cutler thanked her for her business and apologized for any inconvenience, then explained that her husband had made alternative arrangements. The note was clipped to a check—Roni's personal check for the plumbing job, uncashed and marked Void.

Her breath caught, and her throat constricted with a flash of pain that was so blinding, she nearly cried out. Dropping the check as though it scorched her fingertips, she rose from the table, feeling dazed and violated and betrayed.

"Not even that much." Her voice was broken, unrecognizable to her own ears. "Damn you, Sam Preston, you won't even give me that much!"

On the brink of shattering altogether, she reached and found a center of icy calm, closing down on a maelstrom of screaming emotions—anger, hurt, love, fear. She knew with a clarity born of the stripping away of all illusions that life was not fair, that virtue was rarely rewarded and that wishing never, ever made a thing so. Faced with that reality, stripped of choices by her husband's unbending pride, she also knew there was only one trail left to follow.

He found her packing.

"I knew you wouldn't stick it out."

Roni looked up from her suitcase, and her eyes were chilly and faraway. "How very astute of you. And you so love being right."

Sam winced inwardly as she echoed Travis King's words, but his features were frozen, stoic, unrevealing.

He hardly recognized her. Dressed in ballerina flats and a flowing purple gauze dress with lots of artsy jewelry and her hair flowing wild around her head, the Curly he knew was submerged beneath a fashionable West Coast facade. She was much too sophisticated for Flat Fork, Texas, just as he'd known—and feared—all along.

Roni shut the suitcase. The click of the latches made an ominous sound in the bedroom.

"I've arranged for Maria Morales to baby-sit Jessie while I'm gone. They're outside swinging right now, and Maria will be here first thing every morning and stay as late as needed," she said, her voice stony. "I'll catch the red-eye out of DFW tonight. I'll call with the number where I'm staying as soon as I get settled."

"What's the point?"

"The point, Sam, is that I'm going to work for Jackson Dial, not sleep with him." Chin lifted at a haughty angle, she hoisted the suitcase, swept past him and went into the kitchen. "Strangely, he's not the one who insists on treating me like a hooker."

"What the hell's that supposed to mean?" he growled, following her.

She picked up the check from the table and held it out to him. "For services rendered, I presume?"

He took the check, realized what it signified, then tossed it back on the table with a disdainful flick of his wrist. "Damn you, Curly! That doesn't mean anything."

Her jaw worked. "It does to me. And let's get this clear. It's not about the money. It's a symbol of what I can and cannot expect to share with you. But I see now that all you expect, or want, or are even capable of seeing in this relationship is sex and business, and..." Her voice quavered, and she stopped, swallowing hard to regain her composure. "I'm sorry, Sam. I love you, and it's harder than I thought. I don't know if I can settle for so little again. I need some time to think. When I get back, we'll talk."

A claw gripped his heart, squeezed hard, brought on a rising panic that he forced back with harshness. "If you leave now, don't bother to come back."

She stared at him. "You don't mean that."

"The hell I don't."

Her gaze moved from his face to his feet and back again, analyzing him, measuring his character, and finding him wanting. "Then you're a damn fool."

"Two times a loser—I guess you're right." His throat was so thick he thought he'd be sick. "What about Jessie?"

"What about her?" Roni's head snapped around, and there was a flare of anguish and maternal protectiveness in her eyes. "She's as much mine as yours. She's why I'm going. And she's why I'm coming back."

"I told you, don't bother."

Her lashes quivered at that blow; then she raised her eyes and defiantly met his gaze. "You can still change my mind, you know."

His eyes narrowed suspiciously. "And?"

"Tell me you love me, Sam."

His throat closed completely, clogged by misery, stopped up with pride and the fear that she was making a fool of him.

In the silence, she reached for her purse and her suitcase, her features set in lines of resignation, but not surprise. At the door, she paused, but didn't turn to look at him.

"Kiss Jessie good-night for me."

Then she went.

A gaping chasm opened in Sam's soul, but as he looked at the emptiness, he had the satisfaction of knowing that his dignity was unbowed.

## Ten

A frantic scheduling appeal, and by the 15th Sam, no truly understood the toll when "corning back the a horrible. He knew I would and he knew his last word,' prepared for how crazy was?

For the first time in his life, he found no comfort at the dead Diamondy. The influences on his soul slowly, and the filthy collided was a spot telling on cold, with Nick on or even either forlorn silence in the cost that were ever minutes, but knew that their small had... every answer her house. She knew that she once... hard he wasn't so him pains him posted from a level placed to then he the as together, and fathomless in the hundred more it day. Under a of them, Afterwould at last said though? 

His nerve, everyone it that took over that from had... sure to California. Dave now strong feeling and steaks inner a key of down wanted to some... just to as she fathom. He Ant was he he his remembered now he

# Ten

One week stretched into two, and by the third week in June, Sam understood that Roni wasn't coming back. He wasn't surprised. He'd known it would end up this way. He just wasn't prepared for how badly it hurt.

For the first time in his life, he found no comfort at the Lazy Diamond. The house was too big and empty, and his little redhead was mopey, brightening only when "Da-da" appeared, then looking around for the one they were both missing. He knew that Roni called Maria every day about Jessie. He also knew that she never asked to speak to him. Maria had posted Roni's hotel phone number on the refrigerator, and he looked at it a hundred times a day, but he never dialed. What would he have said anyway?

Of course, everyone in Flat Fork knew that Roni had gone to California. Little towns loved gossip, and it hadn't taken a bevy of rocket scientists to connect California with Jackson Dial. And while he hadn't volunteered any details, he'd seen the pity and the curiosity and the accusation in people's eyes.

Even Krystal's concerned expression held an element of censure when she'd come by to kidnap Jessie for the evening. Although she'd had the grace to avoid mentioning Roni, she'd given him some advice.

"You need a break," she'd said. "It's Friday night. Go to town. Take in a movie or something. And don't worry about the baby. My boys are dying to have her spend the night again."

He'd had no intention of taking Krystal's suggestion, preferring to lick his wounds in private, but with Jessie gone, the deserted house was intolerable. Roni's perfume lingered in the bedroom, and visions of her haunted him— asleep on the tumbled bed after a night of loving, laughing at him over the breakfast table, cuddling Jessie to her breast. Those mental pictures had finally chased him from his hole.

Now he slumped in his favorite booth at Rosie's Café, nursing a beer and a bruised ego. Texas honky-tonk music swirled in the smoky air as couples circled the dance floor. Boisterous conversations foamed unnoticed over Sam's head. He studied the label on the bottle and tried not to think.

"Mind if I join you?" A fresh long-neck bottle hit the table in front of Sam. "You look like you could use a friend."

Travis King stood at the edge of the booth, one thumb hooked in the loops beside his championship belt buckle, a canned soft drink in the other hand.

Sam lifted an eyebrow, then shrugged. It was too much trouble to remind Travis that they weren't friends. "Suit yourself."

"Thanks." Travis slid into the opposite bench, then tilted his own drink in a toast. "Cheers."

"*Salut.*" Sam responded in kind. After all, his first bottle was empty and to have done otherwise would have been downright un-Texan. He eyed the soft drink can curiously. "You not having one of these?"

Travis's shoulders lifted beneath his black shirt. "I stay away from the hard stuff these days."

They drank in silence for a while. Finally Travis said, "I hear you got woman trouble. I'm sorry. I like Roni a lot."

Sam shifted off the base of his spine, uncomfortable. "Yeah, well, I never had much luck with women."

Travis wiped a fleck of moisture off his mustache. "Me, neither."

"You?" Sam couldn't hide his skepticism. "You've left a string of broken hearts from Calgary to Brownsville."

"You call that good luck? Being fair game for every buckle bunny from here to the Sierras was fun for a while, but it eventually wears thin, you know what I mean?" Travis shook his head and looked away. "Anyway, it's always the filly who got away who haunts you, especially if it was your own damn fault."

Sam had no comment for that. Taking another pull on his beer, he changed the subject. "You're moving a tad easier these days."

"I'm healing." Travis rotated his shoulder, demonstrating. "Getting out of that sling was a big improvement."

"Still heading for Reno?"

"Yeah. The docs say I ought to quit it, but hell, all I know is rodeoing. What else am I going to do?"

But Sam knew the answer to that. Well, maybe the best man had won. He could give the devil his due, even if it was grudgingly. "Congratulations on landing the deal with Buzz Henry."

Lacing his rope-scarred fingers around his can, Travis blew out a breath. "I let it go."

"What?"

"I couldn't swing it. I got no head for business. Shooting the bull with fellows, okay, but keeping the books straight, figuring out deliveries and still making fifty rodeos a year—no way."

Dumbfounded that Travis had turned down a deal—the one that could have rescued the Lazy Diamond—in such a cavalier fashion, Sam didn't know whether to commiserate with him or punch him in the mouth. "You're mighty calm about it."

"I've had plenty of practice being a screwup." He finished his drink with a sour grimace. "In fact, not much has gone right since the night your brother died."

Perhaps it was his own sensitive state that allowed Sam to hear the bleakness in Travis's words. He looked at the other man, thinking they were much alike, showing a strong and solid front to the world, torn apart on the inside. And for what? Holding on to a grudge, nurturing resentment—what good did it do a man?

"That's a mighty heavy burden to carry," Sam said, his voice quiet. "You want to tell me what happened?"

Travis's expression was startled. "You never wanted to hear—"

"I'm asking now."

Haltingly, Travis spoke of two boys, riding high on their rodeo wins, and too much liquor, a rainy night, lights coming out of nowhere and then the crash...

"Kenny was to hell and gone a better man than me," Travis said finally. His dark eyes were flat and lusterless with painful memories. "Smarter, more guts, good-hearted and the best bull rider I ever saw. He was winning all the big ones already. If I hadn't insisted on driving that night, he'd be the one wearing these championship buckles today, not me."

Sam was silent. Even Travis's success had been tainted by his guilt. But Sam was guilty, too, of being too prideful to see that the other man's pain and grief had matched, if not exceeded, his own. After all, Travis had lost his best friend in that accident. Sam had only recently learned how truly devastating that could be.

Travis was watching him closely, but at Sam's continued silence he began to rise to his feet with a muttered "Oh, hell!"

"Keep your seat, cowboy," Sam ordered. "I got a few things to say."

Reluctance etching his lean features, Travis subsided. His expression said he knew he deserved a cussing and was man enough to take it. "Well, speak your piece."

"Antsy, aren't you?"

Travis's jaw clenched. "I just got better things to do than have my hide peeled by the likes of you."

"Life can sure slam into you sometimes, can't it?" Sam asked conversationally. "Bad things happen, and it's really nobody's fault, and yet we're human and weak and think it'll make us feel better if we can just point the finger."

"So get to the point."

But Sam wouldn't be rushed.

"The real tragedy is when you don't learn from that slap upside the head. Well, I never was too bright or even grown-up about these things, so it's taken me a while, but life's too short to hold on to bitterness. I've been a damn fool, Travis. Kenny's death was a tragic accident. I was wrong to blame you, and you have to stop blaming yourself." Sam offered his hand across the table. "I hope you can forgive me, my friend."

Travis's face reflected his surprise, his confusion, his sudden hope. Swallowing hard, he reached across, and they wrung hands. "There's nothing to forgive."

"There is, but let's cry peace and put it behind us like we should have done years ago."

One corner of Travis's mouth lifted. "Suits me."

"Same here." Sam smiled, a weight lifting that he hadn't even realized he carried. "You want another drink? I'm buying."

"No, but I think I could do some damage to one of Rosie's steaks. How about you?"

"Sounds good."

They flagged down a waitress and placed their orders. While they waited, Sam said thoughtfully, "You know, it's a shame we can't figure out a way to talk Buzz into giving us another crack at that contract."

"Us?" Travis leaned back as the waitress placed platters of man-size sirloin steaks and baked potatoes in front of them. "You mean that?"

"Throwing in together still has possibilities, don't you think?"

"Sure. Always said so myself. Your brains and brawn, my beauty. Helluva combination. Except that you're such a damned stubborn cuss on occasion."

Sam knew Roni would agree with that assessment. "Yeah. Maybe I can turn over a new leaf. To be frank, Travis, I'm almost busted. Landing something with Buzz could save my butt."

"Why didn't you say so?" Travis stuffed a bite of rare steak into his mouth. "But what do we need Buzz for?"

"Huh?"

Travis pointed with the tip of his steak knife. "Look, I got cash coming out my kazoo, but no time or know-how. On the other hand, I got plenty of rodeo contacts and I could sell a boa constrictor a pair of snakeskin boots. You have the rancher's expertise and the management skills to run an operation like this."

"Like what?"

"How's King and Preston Stock Company sound?"

A slow grin split Sam's face, and he began to feel excited. "Damn good. Think we can pull it off?"

"No question. We bypass the middle man and make our own bundle. Partners?" Travis stuck out his hand.

Sam took it again, sealing a gentleman's agreement. "Partners."

They talked particulars until long after there was nothing left on their plates but greasy smears, and the dance floor was empty of all but a single amorous couple. By the time the management turned off the lights and chased them outside to the deserted gravel parking lot, Sam knew that although it might be tight for a while still, the Lazy Diamond would squeak by, thanks to King and Preston Stock Company. Strangely, the triumph he knew he should be feeling didn't materialize. What good was success if Roni wasn't there to share it with him?

The irony of that thought hit him like a loaded eighteen-wheeler. *Sharing.* Wasn't that what Roni had wanted to do? And he'd stonewalled her at every turn out of some mistaken sense of pride and driven her away. Lord, when he made mistakes, they were gargantuan ones.

"Man, what a night." Travis tilted his head back to gaze appreciatively at the panorama of stars shining in the Texas darkness. "Been a lot of places, seen a lot of bright lights, but I don't think there's a prettier spot on earth than right here."

"Some folks I know wouldn't agree."

Travis shot Sam a sharp glance. "Look, I know it isn't my place, but as your new partner I've got a vested interest in your welfare. What the devil's going on with you and Roni, anyway?''

Sam's jaw flexed. "I guess I screwed up."

"Then why are you still standing here?"

"What?"

"She's out in L.A., and you're letting that old boyfriend make time with her. Unless you've decided you don't want her—"

"Hell, no! But . . ."

"Chicken, huh?" Travis grimaced. "Yeah, me, too. I climb aboard two-thousand-pound bulls all day long, but when it comes to leveling with your lady about how you feel—" He shook his head.

"It's not that easy," Sam muttered.

"What? To tell her you love her? You never did, did you?" Travis gave a disgusted snort. "You jackass."

Sam stiffened. "You're treading a fine line there, partner."

"Only because it's the truth." Travis clapped Sam on the shoulder. "I'm speaking from experience, my friend. You've got the same look in your eye that I see in my mirror every morning. It's too late for me, but maybe not for you. *If* you're man enough. Think about it."

Whistling under his breath, Travis sauntered toward his truck. Head reeling, Sam automatically climbed into his own vehicle, reached for the key, then forgot what he was doing. His hands clenched and unclenched around the steering wheel as he wrestled with his own culpability.

Roni had accused him of holding out on her. Had even she realized how much? Because Travis was right—Sam loved her, so much it frightened him to death, so much he'd been incapable of risking his heart to that kind of hurt again. He didn't know when it had happened, but somehow over the years it had taken root, to blossom full-blown under the sunny light of her presence in his house, in his heart, in his life.

He was a jackass, all right. He'd just taken Travis on as a partner, and that was all Roni had ever wanted, to contribute something toward a mutual goal, to be a part of the big picture with him. Why had that been so hard for him to see? Why had he felt so threatened? The answer was in the wide yellow streak running down his spine. But all his cowardice and self-protection and damn-fool pride had earned him was an empty bed, a motherless daughter, an existence that would never be worthwhile or joyous again.

Unless he found the courage to change things. Roni was worth it. Jessie deserved it. But he'd fallen short of the mark in every area so far, so what made him think that he warranted a second chance, or that Roni would even care now? Could he open his heart and risk it all? Could he survive if he didn't? There was really only one answer.

Sam stared into the deep Texas night and wondered if he were man enough for the job.

"I'm telling you, darling, the producers are wild about you."

"And I'm telling you, Jackson, that I'm out of here."

Roni smiled too politely over her champagne flute and wondered what she'd ever seen in this slick tennis-blond filmmaker. Completely unmoved by his emotional pleas for her to stay on just a few more days to consult on another project, she let her attention wander over the crowded room of Beverly Hills party-goers.

Powerful corporate moguls mingled with glamorous starlets. Familiar celebrity faces mixed with unassuming media executives with more influence than the president. Roni figured that there wasn't a diamond or a sequin left on Rodeo Drive.

*Ro-day-o.* What kind of word was that? What was wrong with plain, old-fashioned *rodeo* with down-home Texas folks and lots of good times? And champagne and strawberries out of a paper cup sure beat this fancy crystal—if the company were right. Still, she had to hand it to the host. When Jackson put on a show, he really knew how to do it.

And she was bored stiff. And homesick. And missing Jessie like mad. And as for Sam...

Jackson was wheedling. "So, if you'll just agree to work out this little problem I have—"

"No." Roni kept her expression pleasant, but there was steel in her voice that matched the chunky modern jewelry she wore with her plain black sheath. "You've delayed me long enough. I said I'd shmooze with your bigwigs tonight, and I have, so that's it. Be sure to forward my fee to my agent. It's been nice doing business with you. Excuse me."

Handing a stunned Jackson Dial her glass, she threaded her way through the throngs of the rich and beautiful. She wanted to speak to a couple of people on Jackson's staff who'd been especially helpful. Because, despite the weeks of silence from Flat Fork, despite the hectic schedule to fulfill Jackson's commission, there had been ample opportunity for reflection, and Roni had made her decision. Her heart belonged to Jessie and Sam, and that was where she had to be. She was going home.

Even if Sam never came to love her as she desired, Roni knew now that she had to fight for him, to show him by her actions that she was worthy of his trust and ultimate devotion. Considering Sam's pride, it wouldn't be easy, but she'd find a way to make a life with him. If she were smart and lucky, maybe even a way to break through his shell to the loving man she knew lay underneath.

It was a daunting challenge, fraught with dangers to her heart, and even now the thought of working out their last big disagreement filled her with trepidation and doubt. But they'd made a pact, an agreement to make a home for Jessie, and Roni would keep her part of the bargain to the best of her ability while hoping for the best. What did Corinthians say? *Love beareth all things, believeth all things, hopeth all things.* Loving Sam Preston the way she did, she could give that ideal nothing less that her best. Then, when she came to the end of her life, she would know that it had been worth every effort.

Surrounded elbow to elbow with the gorgeous people in attendance, Roni was speaking to Annie Mitchell, Jackson's dumpy long-suffering secretary, when she realized the older women was no longer listening to her.

"Whoa," Annie murmured, her gaze tracking something behind Roni's head. "Who's the Marlboro Man?"

Roni cast a disinterested glance over her shoulder, then caught her breath. Sun-streaked blond hair, broad shoulders under a leather Western jacket, bluebonnet eyes— Sam! At the same moment her heart leapt in joyful recognition, her eyes narrowed.

For whatever reason he'd materialized at this glitzy function, he appeared to be enjoying himself immensely. Women surrounded him. The brunette in the cut-down-to-there gown clinging to his left arm was practically in heart palpitations, and the California blonde on his right curled her lacquered red nails around his wrist and threw her head back in a trill of laughter calculated to raise any male's libido. Other would-be starlets were stacked three-deep around him, all vying for his attention.

It was Sam's grin that pushed Roni over the edge. Jealousy ignited a flash of claw-curling, female possessiveness.

How dare he induce such a feeding frenzy? Just who did he think he was?

Without making a conscious decision, Roni was moving through the crowd with deadly purpose. Squeezing past a bevy of wannabe cowgirls, she plucked the blonde loose from Sam's sleeve and drove off the brunette with a look like icy marble.

"Back off, ladies. This one's spoken for."

"Curly." Sam's voice was a rumbly Texas drawl, and the crowd of females practically moaned in unison. "I've been looking for you."

"Yeah, I'll bet." With a glare as sharp as a laser beam, Roni dispersed the horde, then dragged Sam by the arm out of the pit of temptation toward a quieter corner where a bank of two-story windows framed a view of the lights twinkling on the Hollywood Hills.

Infuriatingly, Sam was chuckling under his breath. "Whew, now I see what Travis meant about buckle bunnies."

"Don't tell me you weren't enjoying that," Roni snapped. "How'd you get here, anyway?"

Sam jammed his hands into his jeans pockets, his cheek creased in a half smile. "Taxi."

"Don't play games with me," she hissed furiously. "You know what I mean."

"I'm just a simple cowpuncher, ma'am. It's hard for me to think straight when you look so damned beautiful you take my breath."

Roni opened her mouth, then closed it. What was she doing berating Sam like a fishwife when all she really wanted to do was fling herself into his arms? Yet uncertainty stopped her, for she dared not guess why he was here lest she be disappointed. Then a sudden frisson of alarm hit her.

"Is it Jessie? Oh, God, Sam! What's happened? I—"

"No, honey." He took a step closer, slanting his palm over the tumbled fall of her riotous curls in a soothing gesture. "Jessie's fine. Krystal's looking after her."

Roni's lip trembled in equal measures of relief and apprehension. "Then why—?"

"You were right. About Travis and me, that is."

She shook her head. "I don't understand."

"We made our peace."

"Oh, Sam." Wonderment softened her voice. "I'm glad."

"Not only that, but we've decided to throw in together, and I think it's going to plug the hole until the Lazy Diamond's back on its feet."

A sinking sensation lodged in Roni's belly. So he didn't need her money, and all her efforts were for nothing. He'd said all along that he didn't need her help, and he'd been right. Even though it hurt, she was glad for him that the ranch was safe. "That—that's good."

Sam rubbed his jaw. "Yeah, but King and Preston Stock Company is going to need some capital. And seeing how you're a Preston, and I understand you've got some wherewithal to invest, I was thinking..."

Roni could hardly breathe. "What, Sam?"

"That you might want to go in partners. That is, if you can stand being associated with a jackass."

She pressed her fingertips to her quivering mouth, hoping against hope that this olive branch symbolized what she thought it did. "I might manage it, if the return on the investment is high enough."

"Well, there's no guarantees, but the fringe benefits are terrific." Sam slid his hand under her hair and let his callused fingers caress her nape. "I shouldn't have put limits on a free-spirited filly like you, but I was scared."

"You? Of what?"

"Of seeing how you sparkle in this world," he said gravely, indicating the glittery throng with a jerk of his chin. "And of losing you to it. But I think I can get used to sharing you, if you'll just spend a little time with me in mine now and again."

"It's all I've ever wanted."

"Then come home, Roni. Jessie needs you. And I miss you like hell."

Eyes luminous with hope, she looked up into his face. "Why, Sam?"

His laugh was nearly a groan. "You're going to make me say it, aren't you?"

"Only if you can."

He took a deep breath and framed her face between his hands. "I love you, Veronica Jean. And I'm a damn fool for being too stiff-necked and scared to say so before, but it took a good kick in the head to make me realize nothing—not the ranch, not my pride—is worth losing you. I spent the whole plane trip praying it wasn't too late for us."

"You never really lost me, Sam. I was already on my way home, because I love you, too, more than anything."

There was a suspicious glitter in Sam's eyes, and his voice turned husky with emotion. "Aw, hell, Curly, then you'd better come here."

Their kiss was a coming together, a reunion of two hearts rejoicing in new understanding and truth and commitment. Melting, clinging to her man, Roni never wanted it to end. Then again, if things kept progressing, they were going to be putting on a mighty interesting show for Jackson Dial's guests.

Breathless, she pulled back a fraction. "Could we adjourn this to a more private location? I've got a hotel room, complete with room service and a Do Not Disturb sign, and one or two things I'd like to discuss with you."

"I thought you'd never ask, ma'am."

With Roni locked to his side, Sam headed them for the door. She was supremely conscious of the fact that she was the envy of every woman in the room. In fact, she could hear a couple of them gnashing their teeth. It made her want to laugh out loud.

Sam led her outside toward a waiting taxi. "Why the grin?"

"For a man who wasn't sure of himself in this milieu, you certainly have taken the place by storm."

He shrugged. "It's not so bad, I guess."

"Well, I see that I'll have to keep you busy at the ranch for your own safety."

Sam's answering smile was so full of love and promise, it stole Roni's breath. "Curly, I can't wait."

# Epilogue

"**M**ommy, Mommy! Look what I got!"

Sam Preston followed his redheaded daughter as she bounded up the porch steps waving her prize. Nearly three, Jessie was a magpie whose russet curls challenged her mother's patience, for no matter what kind of ribbon or ponytail she used, the little burgeoning tomboy obliterated Roni's efforts within minutes. Carolyn said it was poetic justice, in her opinion, because Roni had been just the same.

Jessie tugged at the handle on the screen door, and Sam paused because she was in her I-can-do-it-myself stage and he knew better than to interfere. It gave him a moment to glance around, noting that the old place had never looked better with its fresh paint and the new addition off the side. A riotous mass of marigolds and geraniums filled the flower beds, and a sign that proclaimed King And Preston Stock Company swung from a post in front of the office they'd installed in the barn. Sam could see Angel Morales, feet propped on his manager's desk, talking on the phone.

Sam's chest swelled with pride and satisfaction. Yes, they'd come a long way in the past two years. Business was good, the ranch was thriving and even old Diablo had sired a string of blooded offspring that was the envy of the county.

But the real miracle to Sam was the way he'd grown inside, from a quiet, needy man afraid to express his longing for tender emotions into, he hoped, a loving person able to communicate intimately with the lady who was his heart, his lover and still his best friend. There was one thing Sam knew for sure: loving Roni had changed his life in every essential way.

Jessie swung the door open, triumph written on her face. "Lookit, Mommy!"

"She's probably in the back," Sam offered. In tiny blue jeans and miniature cowboy boots, Jessie galloped down the hall to the bedroom. Sam peeped around the door frame, and struggled not to laugh. Jessie was bouncing on the bed ninety to nothing, and Roni, apparently fresh out of the bath, stood with her back to him, her curls pinned in a sexy topknot, struggling one-handed into a terry-cloth robe.

"All I wanted was a shower," she moaned. "Was that too much to ask?"

"Having trouble, Curly?"

Roni whirled, infinite gratitude written on her face, and thrust a blanket-wrapped bundle at him. "Oh, thank heavens. Here, Sam, take your son."

Sam accepted the infant, smiling down into the chubby face and tickling his chin with a forefinger. At two months, he was growing like a weed and destined someday to be his father's size. "Has Tommy been giving you a hard time, honey?"

"You'd never know it to look at the little angel now that *Thomas* was giving me the very devil five minutes ago, would you?"

Sam grinned and stroked the fine down sprouting at his son's nape. "You know something? I swear we've got us another redhead."

"I think you could be right. Scary, huh?" Roni swept Jessie up off the bed and whirled her in a circle. "And what did I tell you about jumping on my bed, young lady? How's Mommy's big girl?"

"Look!" Jessie insisted, thrusting the book she held at her mother's nose. "Daddy says it's mine."

"Omigosh! It came." Wondering, Roni plopped down in the rocking chair with Jessie on her lap, thumbing through the colorful pages. "It's beautiful."

"My name," Jessie insisted, pointing to the cover. "Daddy said so."

"And he's absolutely right, darling." Roni smothered her daughter's brow with exuberant kisses, then read the title. "*Jessie's Critters*. Written and illustrated by your mommy."

"Congratulations, Curly," Sam said, squatting by the rocker to admire her creation. Settling Tommy against his shoulder, he leaned over and kissed her. "It's great."

"Mmm." Pouting slightly, she gave him a sultry look. "It sure is. Could you do that again?"

"Better not," he teased. "Might lead to something."

"I'm counting on it, cowboy."

Sam laughed, his heart full of the wonder of this happy moment. "Know something, Curly?"

"What, Sam?"

"I'm the luckiest cowpuncher on earth."

And he kissed her again to prove it.

\* \* \* \* \*

# COMING NEXT MONTH

## MILLION DOLLAR SWEEPSTAKES (III)

No purchase necessary. To enter, follow the directions published. Method of entry may vary. For eligibility, entries must be received no later than March 31, 1996. No liability is assumed for printing errors, lost, late or misdirected entries. Odds of winning are determined by the number of eligible entries distributed and received. Prizewinners will be determined no later than June 30, 1996.

Sweepstakes open to residents of the U.S. (except Puerto Rico), Canada, Europe and Taiwan who are 18 years of age or older. All applicable laws and regulations apply. Sweepstakes offer void wherever prohibited by law. Values of all prizes are in U.S. currency. This sweepstakes is presented by Torstar Corp., its subsidiaries and affiliates, in conjunction with book, merchandise and/or product offerings. For a copy of the Official Rules send a self-addressed, stamped envelope (WA residents need not affix return postage) to: MILLION DOLLAR SWEEPSTAKES (III) Rules, P.O. Box 4573, Blair, NE 68009, USA.

## EXTRA BONUS PRIZE DRAWING

No purchase necessary. The Extra Bonus Prize will be awarded in a random drawing to be conducted no later than 5/30/96 from among all entries received. To qualify, entries must be received by 3/31/96 and comply with published directions. Drawing open to residents of the U.S. (except Puerto Rico), Canada, Europe and Taiwan who are 18 years of age or older. All applicable laws and regulations apply; offer void wherever prohibited by law. Odds of winning are dependent upon number of eligibile entries received. Prize is valued in U.S. currency. The offer is presented by Torstar Corp., its subsidiaries and affiliates in conjunction with book, merchandise and/or product offering. For a copy of the Official Rules governing this sweepstakes, send a self-addressed, stamped envelope (WA residents need not affix return postage) to: Extra Bonus Prize Drawing Rules, P.O. Box 4590, Blair, NE 68009, USA.

SWP-S895

## SILHOUETTE®
## Desire® Hearts of Stone

Three strong-willed Texas siblings whose rock-hard
protective walls are about to come tumblin' down!

The Silhouette Desire miniseries by

**BARBARA McCAULEY**
continues with

August 1995

**TEXAS TEMPTATION** (Silhouette Desire #948)
Jared Stone had lived with a desperate guilt. Now he
had a shot to make everything right again—until the
one woman he couldn't have became the only woman
he wanted.

Then read the conclusion in December 1995 with:

**TEXAS PRIDE** (Silhouette Desire #971)
Raised with a couple of overprotective brothers,
Jessica Stone *hated* to be told what to do. So when
her sexy new foreman started trying to run her life,
Jessica's pride said she had to put a stop to it. But
her heart said something *entirely* different....

And if you missed **TEXAS HEAT** (Silhouette Desire
#917), the first book in the *Hearts of Stone* trilogy,
be sure to order your copy today!

Rugged rancher Jake Stone had just found out that he
had a long-lost half sister—and he was determined to
get to know her. Problem was, her legal guardian and
aunt, sultry Savannah Roberts, was intent on keeping
him at arm's length.

# As a *Privileged Woman,*
## you'll be entitled to all
## these *Free Benefits.*
## And *Free Gifts, too.*

To thank you for buying our books, we've designed an exclusive FREE program called *PAGES & PRIVILEGES™.* You can enroll with just one Proof of Purchase, and get the kind of luxuries that, until now, you could only read about.

## *B*IG HOTEL DISCOUNTS

**A privileged woman stays in the finest hotels.** And so can you—at up to 60% off! Imagine standing in a hotel check-in line and watching as the guest in front of you pays $150 for the same room that's only costing you $60. Your *Pages & Privileges* discounts are good at Sheraton, Marriott, Best Western, Hyatt and thousands of other fine hotels all over the U.S., Canada and Europe.

## *F*REE DISCOUNT TRAVEL SERVICE

**A privileged woman is always jetting to romantic places.** When <u>you</u> fly, just make one phone call for the lowest published airfare at time of booking—<u>or double the difference back!</u> PLUS—

you'll get a $25 voucher to use the first time you book a flight AND <u>5% cash back on every ticket you buy thereafter through the travel service!</u>

SD-PP4A

# FREE GIFTS!

**A privileged woman is always getting wonderful gifts.**
Luxuriate in rich fragrances that will stir your senses (and his). This gift-boxed assortment of fine perfumes includes three popular scents, each in a beautiful designer bottle. <u>Truly Lace</u>...This luxurious fragrance unveils your sensuous side. <u>L'Effleur</u>...discover the romance of the Victorian era with this soft floral. <u>Muguet des bois</u>...a single note floral of singular beauty.

# FREE INSIDER TIPS LETTER

**A privileged woman is always informed.** And you'll be, too, with our free letter full of fascinating information and sneak previews of upcoming books.

# MORE GREAT GIFTS & BENEFITS TO COME

**A privileged woman always has a lot to look forward to.** And so will you. You get all these wonderful FREE gifts and benefits now with only one purchase...and there are no additional purchases required. However, each additional retail purchase of Harlequin and Silhouette books brings you a step closer to even more great FREE benefits like half-price movie tickets... and even more FREE gifts.

*L'Effleur*...This basketful of romance lets you discover L'Effleur from head to toe, heart to home.

*Truly Lace*...
A basket spun with the sensuous luxuries of Truly Lace, including Dusting Powder in a reusable satin and lace covered box.

*Complete the Enrollment Form in the front of this book and mail it with this Proof of Purchase.*

PROOF OF PURCHASE

Offer expires October 31, 1996

SD-PP4